Raves For the
LAWRENCE BLOCK!

Shank was being followed. He heard the footsteps behind him and saw the figure over his left shoulder. Shank's first reactions were automatic. He stopped abruptly, wheeled, headed across the street and doubled back along the block. As Shank turned he spotted a man wearing a grey overcoat and a felt hat shading his face.

All right. Shank had a tail. Now he had to keep the tail from realizing that his presence had been detected. If the tail knew Shank was on to him, the whole game would become that much harder.

Shank strode down First to Saint Marks, pacing at his usual speed. He turned at the corner, spotting the tail again as he did so, and headed toward his own building.

Then he took the stairs two at a time, wondering how long the tail would stay on the street before he decided to have a look inside.

He closed the door, sliding the bolt into place. Then he raced around the apartment, grabbing the half-empty brown envelope from the table, snatching up the packet of cigarette papers although there was nothing illegal about owning them, picking up also the sack of Bull Durham on the off chance some pot was mixed in with the tobacco. He hadn't remembered spicing up that particular sack but there was no point taking chances.

The toilet worked on the first flush for the first time in a good three weeks. He flushed it again for the sheer hell of it and let himself relax completely for the first time since he had spotted the tail.

The relaxation did not last. Suppose Joe had left a roach some place around? Christ, all the cops needed was a grain of the stuff and they could stick you with possession if they wanted you badly enough. Suppose the son of a—

A knock sounded at the door.

"Open up there. Police..."

A DIET of TREACLE

by **Lawrence Block**

A HARD CASE CRIME NOVEL

A HARD CASE CRIME BOOK

(HCC-039)

First Hard Case Crime edition: January 2008

Published by

Titan Books
A division of Titan Publishing Group Ltd
144 Southwark Street
London
SE1 0UP

in collaboration with Winterfall LLC

ISBN 978-0-85768-304-5

Cover design by Cooley Design Lab
Design direction by Max Phillips
www.maxphillips.net

Typeset by Swordsmith Productions

The name "Hard Case Crime" and the Hard Case Crime logo
are trademarks of Winterfall LLC. Hard Case Crime books are
selected and edited by Charles Ardai.

Printed and bound by CPI Group (UK) Ltd, Croydon, CR0 4YY

Visit us on the web at www.HardCaseCrime.com

To all stoop-sitters, everywhere…

A DIET OF TREACLE

"Once upon a time there were three little sisters,"
the Dormouse began in a great hurry;
"and their names were Elsie, Lacie, and Tillie;
and they lived at the bottom of a well—"

"What did they live on?" said Alice, who always took
a great interest in questions of eating and drinking.

"They lived on treacle," said the Dormouse.

"They couldn't have done that, you know," Alice
gently remarked. "They'd have been ill."

"So they were," said the Dormouse. "Very ill."

—FROM ALICE IN WONDERLAND

1

Joe Milani studied the room with half-open eyes. He spent a long time absorbing every aspect of the interior of the coffee-house with the intensity of a person who had never been there before and who might never return. At last he rested his gaze on the small cup of coffee in front of him with the same concentration. And he decided that the coffee-house was the most logical spot in the world for him.

Item one: the name of the place was The Palermo—after the city in which his grandfather had been born.

Item two: the coffee-house had a Bleecker Street address—the street on which his father had been born.

Item three: the coffee-house belonged to the fringe of Greenwich Village—where all the world's misfits were supposed to live. And he thought that he, Joe Milani, one of humanity's round pegs, had found the world the squarest of holes.

He laughed to himself, pleased at his play on words. Then, chopping off his laugh as suddenly as he had started it, he raised the demitasse of espresso to his lips. He took a sip, savoring the thick, black liquid. Thirty cents was what The Palermo picked up for a cup of espresso, thirty cents for a squirt of ink, thirty shining coppers for a less-than-respectable swallow of liquid mud. Joe's grandfather, who might well have sipped espresso in the same chair before coffee-houses had become fashionable, had probably paid a nickel for the slop.

Thirty cents. But, Joe reflected, as he swallowed the coffee, that gummy concoction was worth it. If you were stoned, that is.

Stoned. He was that. Stoned, smashed, blind, turned on and flying so high and so cool and everything so just exactly right.

Softly he sang:

Every time it rains, it rains
Sweet marijuana.
I grow pot in my backyard,
Sweet marijuana.
Sweet marijuana.
I blow up in my garage
Any time I wanna…

Joe Milani looked across the table at Shank to see if the guy was digging the song, if the thin boy of the intense black eyes and the straight black hair would nod and mumble and laugh with him. But Shank was cooling it, his eyes shut, his hand supporting his chin. Shank, stoned, was listening in to something and digging something—maybe some music he had heard weeks ago or a chick he had balled or maybe nothing but his own private thoughts.

Joe took another bite out of the espresso, marveling at the way everything tasted so much better when you were high. It was as if you were getting the whole taste, inside and out, and as if, were you to close your eyes, you could see what you were eating. He felt that his lips tasted the coffee, and then flipped the liquid to his tongue and palate; and then, when he swallowed it he was convinced that his throat could taste the coffee as it made its way to his stomach. He finally finished the espresso and leaned back against the wrought iron chair, his eyelids low and his hands motionless in his lap. He was tuning in on himself.

Deliberately he concentrated on his right hand. He could see the hand vividly in his mind, the dark curling hairs on its back, the whorls on the fingertips. He could feel the pulse in his hand, and the blood moving through the palm into the fingers. His hand grew very heavy, throbbing as he concentrated on it.

Joe shifted his concentration from one part of his body to another, and each time the effect was the same. His heart pounded and was bright red in his mind's eye. His lungs swelled and flattened as he breathed in and out.

Cool.

So cool…

How long had it been? Two joints a few minutes after noon, two joints he and Shank had split, two little cigarettes hand-rolled in wheat-straw paper and smoked rapidly, had been passed back and forth between them until there had been nothing left but two roaches, two tiny butts that they had stuffed into the hollowed-out ends of regular cigarettes and had smoked the same way. Just two joints—and they had gotten so stoned, so fly, that it seemed now as if the high were going to go on forever.

With an effort Joe pushed open his eyes and straightened up in the chair. The good thing about pot was that you could turn yourself on and off and on again and never lose control—unlike beer or wine or whiskey that rocked you only to dull everything finally. And pot had it all over heroin or morphine or cocaine—the hard stuff that sent you on the nod and left you in a fog until it wore off and you were down on the ground.

No, Joe Milani weightily concluded, pot was so much better. No habit, no hangover, no loss of control. And it didn't take more and more of the stuff to get you high each time, no matter what the books said, because the books were all written by people who didn't know, people who hadn't been there. Joe had been there, and he was there right now, and he knew.

And he idly wondered what the time would tell him.

There was a clock on the wall behind the cash register. By squinting, he could just about make out the numbers—nearly 3:30, which meant that he had been high for better than three hours on two little joints. And the three hours felt like at least six, because when you were high you noticed everything that was happening and the time crawled by and let you stroke it on its furry back.

He glanced at Shank, who hadn't moved since Joe's benevolent eye had last fallen on him. Then Milani gazed around the coffee-house again—and saw the girl.

She was extremely pretty. Joe dwelled a long time on the girl, taking careful note of the brown hair verging on black, long lovely hair falling very neatly to her shoulders. He studied the full mouth slightly reddened by lipstick, and the clean, small hands whose slender fingers curled around the sides of a cup of cappucino. Her enormous eyes were enhanced by a clear and lightly tanned complexion, and her bare forearms, covered by downy hair, were neither too heavy nor too thin. Joe searched her face, hoping she wouldn't turn toward him while he examined her. He tried to see through her, into her.

She appeared to be out of place in The Palermo. Her simple attire of white blouse, dark green skirt and flats was appropriate enough for a Villager, but there was an aura about her that made Joe certain she didn't live in the area.

She was hardly more than a few tables away from him, sitting alone at the window, and doing nothing but looking pretty. But doing that quite well indeed.

Joe leaned across the table and shook Shank by the shoulder. At first he aroused no response; then Shank's eyes slitted and his features assumed a what-the-hell-is-it-now expression.

"Man—" Joe Milani began.

"Yeah?"

"Dig." Joe nodded in the direction of the girl. Shank flicked, then turned back.

"The chick?" Shank barely made the question.

Joe managed his head up and down a half inch either way.

"What about her?"

"Watch, man. I'm going to pick her up."

Shank took in the sight of the girl again, more closely this time. Then he shrugged.

"You won't make it, man," he said.

"You don't think so?"

Shank shook his head slowly, his eyes dreamy, his face completely relaxed again. When he spoke, the words were spaced wide apart and enunciated precisely, as if he were rolling each syllable on his tongue in order to taste it.

"Never, man. She is a pretty chick and like that, but she is also a very square chick and she will put you into the ground if you so much as say hello to her. She will put you down so hard you will have to crawl back to the table, man. On your knees, like."

Joe giggled softly.

"Go ahead," Shank said. "Try, if you have eyes. But you won't make it."

"Look, I'm stoned, Shank."

"So what?"

Joe giggled again. "Don't you dig, Shank? I'm blind, and when I'm blind I become very cool. I say everything just right and I play everything off the wall and I never strike out, man. I'm just so cool."

He repeated "cool," dragging out the word so he could feel just how cool he was, how clear-headed and icily calm.

"You just think you're cool," Shank said. "You'll scare the girl, baby. You'll scare her and she'll put you down."

"Why do you put it there?"

"That's where it's at."

Joe smiled, a lazy smile. "Bet me," he said. "Bet me I don't pick her up."

"What do you want to bet?"

He considered. "Bet me a joint," he offered.

"A joint?"

Joe nodded.

"Cool," Shank said. "I got a joint you don't get to first base."

"You'll lose the bet, baby. Us wops never lose a bet, you know. Especially when we're high."

He did not wait for Shank to reply. Instead, he stood up, light on his feet, calm. He was extremely sure of himself, sure he was tall and good-looking enough to attract her, sure he would come on strong enough to interest her. He was twenty-seven, which meant he had a good five years on the girl at the very least, and he was a little more than six feet tall—wide-shouldered, narrow-waisted and muscular. He rubbed the palm of one hand over his cheek, glad he had taken the trouble to shave this morning.

But he wasn't dressed very well, he realized—just dirty chinos and a t-shirt. Besides, his crew-cut had grown out to the point where he ought to start combing it or have it cut again. But he felt so cool, so utterly cool, that all the rest didn't matter.

He walked to the girl's table, slowly, easily, his eyes fixed on her face. She did not peer up, not even when he stood over her to stare down at her so intensely he was certain she must have been aware of his presence.

Then he drummed a tattoo on the table-top. Startled, she raised her eyes.

"Hello," he said, pleasantly. "Is your name Bernice?"

A second or two elapsed before she could reply. At last she shook her head rapidly.

"I didn't think it was," he said. "Neither is mine."

She said nothing, her expression one of bewilderment.

"You look awfully familiar," he said, pushing onward. "Have you ever been in Times Square?"

"Why I—"

"Great place, Tunes Square. Did you ever stop to think that there's a phrenology parlor on Eighth Avenue that opens 4:30 in the morning?"

Wide-eyed, lips parted, she seemed prettier than ever.

"I know what you're doing," he confided. "You've got the rest of these people fooled but I'm wise to you. They think you're just drinking a cup of cappuccino but I know for a fact you're planning the Portuguese invasion."

He waited for that to sink in, wondering at the same time what in the world he was talking about. Then he flashed her a great smile and fastened one hand on the chair opposite her. She tried to say something but he beat her to it, timing everything with intuitive flawlessness.

"You're very pretty," he said, "even if your name isn't Bernice and you've never been to Times Square and you don't happen to be planning the Portuguese invasion. You don't mind if I sit down, do you?"

For a moment she gave the impression of speech-lessness, as if lost somewhere in left field, he thought, and he was on the point of sitting down without waiting for a reply when she finally managed utterance.

"Go ahead," she said. "I mean…you probably would anyway, wouldn't you?" He pulled back the chair and sat down, longing to glance at Shank triumphantly. Instead, he smiled at the girl.

"If you're name isn't Bernice, what is it?" Joe Milani inquired.

"Oh," she said. "It's Anita."

"Hello, Anita."

"Hello."

"Do you live here in the Village, Anita?" He knew that she didn't but it was as good a question as any.

"No, I'm just visiting."

"Where do you live?"

"Uptown."

"Uptown," he said, "takes in a lot of ground."

"116th Street between Second and Third."

"Yeah? Way up in wop Harlem?"

She stiffened.

"What's the matter?" He put the question with some concern.

"Do you have to use that word?"

"What word?" It was hard to avoid laughing but he made it.

"Wop," she said softly. "I don't like that word."

This time he let himself smile. "I am called Joseph Milani," he said in perfect Italian. In English he added, "So it is all right if I use the word?"

Anita, by now off-balance, was attempting to say something but she obviously had not the slightest idea of what it should be, so her mouth moved soundlessly. Confidently, he reached out a hand and let the fingertips touch hers.

She neither drew away nor flinched.

He examined her again. He decided her body was exceptionally good, decidedly not a trial to behold, a little on the slender side but starring breasts firm and well-shaped.

Joe considered he had her practically hypnotized. He said a silent prayer of thanks to the pot, flashed her a smile showing his white teeth, and pressed her fingers gently.

"Anita," he said, "The Palermo is a pleasant place, but it's too hot and too stuffy and too limited. Let's make it."

"Make it?"

"Split," he said. "Cut out. Leave."

"Oh."

"Come on," he said. He stood up; mesmerized, she stood up, too. He waited while she paid her check. Then she rejoined him, and he took her hand in his.

Her hand felt very soft, but he resisted the temptation to give it a gentle squeeze. Leading her out of the coffee-house, he glanced at Shank.

But Shank was in another world, his head lolling back, his eyes veiled, and one hand lying limp on the table before him like a discarded napkin.

2

Leon Marsten, whom nobody had called anything but Shank for the last four years, sat up abruptly at four-seventeen P.M. and blinked rapidly. He fumbled for a cigarette and lit it. Laboriously, he dragged smoke into his lungs and held it there. He blew it out slowly in a long, thin column that floated languidly toward the ceiling. When he finished the cigarette, he dropped it and elaborately ground it into the linoleum with the heel of his tennis shoe until it was completely shredded.

The ritual completed, he turned and methodically surveyed the coffee shop. Satisfied that nobody was watching him, he stood up and strode out the door onto Bleecker Street.

To hell with The Palermo, he thought—the coffee was on the house for a change.

He walked west on Bleecker, moving quickly but not really in a hurry. At Macdougal Street he turned uptown and walked past coffee-houses and restaurants and gift shops toward Washington Square Park. Once in the park, he paused to drink at the water fountain. A little later, he stopped again to buy an ice cream sucker from one of the Good Humor Men haunting the Square, and resumed his stride as he ate his ice cream.

He halted at an empty park bench near the circle at the foot of Fifth Avenue, and sat down. From the back pocket of his dungarees he pulled a paperback novel. He relaxed on the bench and turned the pages of the book.

Shank was twenty years old. He had been born little more than twenty years before to Jeff and Lucy Marsten who, not long after the boy's birth, had mutually agreed to a divorce. Jeff Marsten had then married a girl named Susan Lockridge, the two remaining in El Cajon, California, while Lucy and her son had moved to Berkeley where, in no time at all, Lucy had once again become a bride, this time to a Mr. Bradley Galton. Shortly thereafter, Mr. and Mrs. Galton, son Leon in tow, had pulled up stakes to settle in Los Angeles.

But Leon—Shank—had developed an instant and abiding dislike for the fat and ruddy Bradley Galton. Shank had tried to compensate for his deepening hatred toward his stepfather by intensifying what he had at first felt to be love for his mother; but Shank's love evidently could not have run too deep, because the fact that his mother had married Bradley had been enough to mock the boy's desire to feel more affectionate toward her, and the more he had thought about that, the less delight had he felt in her presence. And after she had given birth to a baby girl, Cindy, Shank could feel no affection for his mother at all.

For that matter, Shank had not liked anybody, not until much, much later.

He grew up alone, a quiet, moody boy who went his own way and thought his own thoughts. He was more clever than intelligent, but his grades in school concealed the fact neatly. School was a challenge for him, not to work, but to avoid work and cause trouble. In the beginning he displayed no particular imagination at causing trouble. When he played with other children, in the days when there were still other children who would play with him, he broke their toys or fought with them or beat them up. He was always short and always thin, but his wiry frame and superb coordination won him every fight. On the other hand, it should also be mentioned that he never took on a fight unless he could count on victory.

Growing older, he grew more inventive. All through grammar school, Halloween was a special treat for him, but he never played the game the way it was supposed to be played. The other children in the neighborhood gave homeowners the option of trick-or-treat; Shank dispensed with the treats and soaped windows. That was the first year. The second year he observed Halloween he realized that playing the trick did not have to rule out the treat. He collected a huge bagful of candy that year. He also broke fifteen windows and slashed two tires with a paring knife he stole from the kitchen.

After that he habitually carried the paring knife in an improvised sheath. When he was fourteen he threw the paring knife into a sewer—he had purchased a switchblade, a well-made stiletto whose six-inch blade of keenly honed steel sprang instantly into position at the touch of the proper button.

Shank could not seem to stay out of trouble, and his stepfather, Bradley Galton, was constantly fishing him out. Shank committed shoplifting, vandalism, smoking in school—anything minor or major. After the boy's second arrest for stealing, from which he was released once again into Bradley Galton's custody, the judge recommended psychiatric treatment.

Bradley Galton thought that an excellent idea. So did Lucy. A psychiatrist was consulted and an appointment set up for Shank.

Shank ridiculed the whole idea. He never kept the appointment.

A month before his sixteenth birthday Shank met the first people he found he could like. There were about twenty of them, slum kids, members of a gang called the Royal Ramblers. And they liked Shank.

They provided him with his name, a name he could get a lot more high on than Leon. They named him Shank because of the knife he always carried and the way he dug it. After the Royal Ramblers gave him the name, he refused to answer to Leon.

They also provided him with his first woman. A broken-down, feeble-minded thing the Royal Ramblers kept around for utility, but she had a passable face, a willing body and she knew how to knock off the one thing she was good for. Shank took her on a mattress on the Ramblers' clubhouse floor, a vacant basement room on San Pedro Street, while four other boys waited their turns.

Shank enjoyed the girl. Sex had been a mystery and one to which he had not paid too much attention. There had been no friends to talk with or tell dirty jokes to. He had waited, and now he knew what sex was all about.

Naturally, other girls followed. What Shank lacked in handsomeness was made up for by his startling black hair and eyes in brilliant contrast to skin white as death, and his catlike walk enhanced the general hypnotic quality. He was usually successful with the girls who hung out with the Ramblers, and if a girl had any reservations all he had to do was show her the knife. He would take it from his pocket, snap the button and the girl's eyes would fasten on the long blade of cold steel.

He never actually had to use the knife on a girl. He never had to play things the least bit rough, for that matter, because the combination of his cold, black eyes in a cold, white face coupled with his showing of six inches of cold steel was enough to warm any of the girls he met. And he liked the way they responded after he showed them the knife. Sometimes he would display the knife to a girl already willing to yield to him.

Friendship, a name, sex and marijuana—these were the gifts of the Ramblers. They were the gifts Shank wanted, too, and he indulged himself for the next two-and-a-half years. He dropped out of high school as soon as he passed the compulsory education age limit and he lived on the streets with his friends. His home was a place to eat breakfast at mid-morning and to sleep at night. He ate the rest of his meals at lunch counters on Fifth Street and spent the rest of his time doing next to nothing.

Shank was nineteen when his girl announced she was pregnant.

She wasn't simply a nice roll in the hay, this girl. She was two years younger than Shank, a virgin when he'd met her, a pretty half-Mexican of almond-shaped eyes and a full-blown figure. She slept with him when he wanted her and spent time with him when he tolerated her presence.

At no time did she expect Shank to marry her; she knew better. Neither did she want to have a baby, so she asked him to give her money for an abortion. There was this doctor a friend of hers knew, she explained, and he would perform an abortion for two hundred dollars.

Shank considered the matter quite carefully. An abortion cost two hundred dollars, but a plane ticket to New York City cost less than half that sum. Simple economics, and a long-present desire to live in New York, influenced Shank to board a plane three days later as he wondered how long it would be before his mother missed the hundred and fifty dollars he had stolen from her.

He never left New York thereafter. A day after his arrival he settled in a single room on Rivington Street on the Lower East Side, a roach-infested cell without a sink and featuring one sagging bed for furniture. The condition of the room could not repel Shank as long as it rented at four dollars a week.

Still, money threatened to be a problem. The thought of a job occurred to him and he went so far as to buy a paper to glance through the classified section. He noted the jobs he thought he might be able to obtain, their hours, pay and type of work, and he promptly rolled up the paper and flipped it out the window. That was the last he thought about jobs.

A day or so later he drifted west to Greenwich Village and wandered around. He met a girl who managed to deploy him into a conversation. She was several years older than he, and a little overweight.

She thought Shank interesting. He thought her stupid.

But before night sank into morning he had borrowed ten dollars from her, bought half an ounce of marijuana, taken her back to his room and made hectic love to her. Then she hurried back to the Bronx where she lived with her mother and father. When she returned the next afternoon he threw her out. She tried a second time, so he showed her the knife and explained in a confidential tone if she ever annoyed him again he would stick the knife in her stomach. As he pointed out the risk, his eyes were half-closed and his lips slightly curved. The plump girl tried to laugh, but it emerged as a hiccup.

He never saw her again.

At first Shank missed the Royal Ramblers. He made vague overtures to the neighborhood gang but they were Puerto Ricans, so he made no supreme efforts to work his way in. Besides, he was older than they were.

By the end of the first week New York began to bore him. He took what marijuana he had left, cut it with a sack of Bull Durham, rolled the result and peddled it at half-a-buck a cigarette. This gave him a little more capital, but money remained tight. The upshot was that he went down to the draft board to enlist.

He could never determine just why he tried to join the army. In any case, he was rejected because the psychiatrist decided Shank was psychopathic, naturally withholding the information. At the time, the army appealed to Shank, perhaps because he felt a little lonely and out of place. But then he discovered there were others like himself, and he was glad the army had turned him down.

There weren't that many—of the others. You could walk all over the Village and never notice them, not unless you were one yourself and consequently knew what to look for. They varied in age, appearance and dress, but a boy like Shank knew how to spot them.

They were lost people, bored people, tired people, angry young people, zen people, beat people. They were tagged with more labels than you could shake a stick of pot at, but the people themselves scorned the labels and spent little time worrying about them. Shank himself shrugged at labels. He knew there were two classes of people in the world—the ones he liked and the ones he didn't.

The ones he didn't could go in a body to hell, as far as he was concerned. The ones he liked were going to hell, too, but he happened to be going on the same boat they were—and that made the difference.

The people he gravitated to smoked marijuana or gobbled benzedrine or drank cough syrup or chewed peyote. They talked with each other, walked with each other, sat with each other and slept with each other. They listened to jazz, deep and grinding hard bop, and they spoke their own language, the inner language of Hip.

There was Lee Revzin, an anemic-looking young man whose hair was forever falling into his eyes, sandy blond hair he neither cut nor combed. Lee wrote poetry, weird stuff Shank found impossible to understand, but he knew the poetry had Soul and if that was Lee's scene it was okay with him.

There was Judy Obershain of the china-doll face, a small, cute, nervous girl who talked and moved like a Disney cartoon. She had experienced sexual relations with forty-seven men, but although the carnal in its many forms attracted Judy, the idea of pain she was convinced was associated with the loss of virginity was the one prospect that terrified her. Shank took her to his room one night but left her virginity where he found it, practically untouched. He thought she was a little nuts, but if that was her scene it was okay with him. Because she was one of Shank's people.

And there were many others. The ones who lived in the Village or on the lower East Side. The ones who lived uptown or in Brooklyn or the Bronx or Queens or even Jersey and who came to the Village to meet the rest. The ones who blew in from Chicago or the coast, the ones who left and the ones who came back. People who wrote or painted or who did nothing at all. Negroes who slept with whites in the frantic shift to change the color of their skins; and whites who slept with Negroes for the opposite shift.

And Joe, of course. Joe Milani, Shank's friend, older than most of the others, who once had been to Korea and to college and who now had no scene at all—who just floated, never wanting anything, never needing anything, just drifting and tasting and touching and seeing and smelling and hearing, drifting around and digging everything, going nowhere and doing nothing. He and Joe lived together now on Saint Marks Place near Avenue A, and the two of them were very tight.

Joe was older, seven years older, but his age did not matter. Joe was a wop, but there was a world of difference between Joe and the dago bastards who owned everything in the Village. Joe was a little nuts in some ways, but Shank did not sit in judgment.

That was Joe's scene, and Shank let it go at that.

The man Shank was expecting sat down next to him. The man wore a white shirt open at the neck and a pair of grey gabardine trousers. The man was nervous.

"Are you Shank?" he said.

Shank nodded.

"Are you holding?"

"I never hold, man."

The man hesitated. "Phil told me—"

"Phil?"

"Phil Carroway. Short guy with a goatee."

Shank nodded again, remembering Phil Carroway.

"He said—"

"I never hold," Shank said. "I've got some stuff back at my pad, if you've got the time."

"Where do you live?"

Shank told him.

"I'd like to get some."

Shank turned and studied the man out of the corner of his eye. Well-dressed, clean-shaven, eager as a sixteen-year-old at a whorehouse for the first time. A Madison Avenue type trying to be hip, looking for a kick and ready to pay for it. Square as they come, but his wallet was full and he would pay good money for a few joints.

Shank stood up. The man hesitated, then rose and

stood next to him awkwardly. "Let's make it," Shank said. "It's a long walk."

"We can take a cab," the man said. "I'll pay for it."

Shank nodded shortly and they walked over to Fifth where the man flagged a taxi. The man held the door for him and Shank hopped in, sinking heavily into the seat.

The square had bread, heavy bread, if he was ready to lay out cab fare just to make a buy, Shank decided. The square was going to be profitable, he decided.

3

Shank held the cigarette paper between the thumb and index finger of his left hand. He poured marijuana into the paper from a small brown envelope. When the paper held a sufficient quantity, he rolled it expertly, wetting the gummed edge by a flick of his tongue, then twisting the ends so the marijuana would not dribble out.

Then he took the cigarette once again between the thumb and the index finger of his left hand and examined it thoughtfully. He held it to the light, checking for possible punctures in the paper. Putting it to his lips, Shank drew on it experimentally to make sure it would smoke properly.

Then he tossed it across the room to Joe Milani, who caught it one-handed, studied it momentarily, and dropped it into his pocket.

"Did you score?" Shank said.

Joe shook his head.

"What happened?"

Joe thought for a minute. Then he shrugged. "I picked her up is all. Picked her up and won the bet."

"How come you didn't ball her?"

"I don't know."

Shank said nothing. The guy never pried, Joe

thought. He was a clever son of a bitch—he just sat
there waiting and pretty soon you told him whatever it
was he was waiting to hear. Non-directive as all hell.

"I don't know," Joe said again.

Shank remained silent.

There were so many things you didn't know, Joe
thought, and it was such a general pain to bother
trying to think things out, especially when there was
no point—thinking them out to begin with.

"Name's Anita Carbone," Joe said. "Lives up in wop
Harlem with her grandmother."

Shank shrugged.

"College chick," Joe continued. "Psych major at
Hunter, comes downtown once every third blue moon."

"Pretty chick."

"Yeah."

More silence.

"Look, I didn't even try to make it with her," Joe
said. "I don't think I could have if I tried, and it's like
there's no future in it anyway. She's a nice square little
thing with a good head and a good body and that's all."

"Where did you take her?"

"Around. We walked around for a while and sort of
talked at each other. After a while I let her buy me a
hamburger at Riker's. Then I put her on a subway and
she zipped off to Harlem and I came down here.
That's all."

"You gonna see her again?"

"No."

"No?"

Joe frowned. "What for, man? Like I told you—she's a nice square little chick and all and we have nothing to talk about and nothing to do. So what for?"

Shank let it drop. "I worked a deal while you were walking around with her," he said.

"Yeah?"

"I sold some cut-down stuff to a Madison Avenue type for more than it was worth."

"What did you get?"

"Twenty cents for twelve."

A cent was a dollar in hip parlance. Twenty cents was twenty dollars, twenty dollars for maybe four or five dollars worth of pot. Joe whistled.

"He's happy," Shank said. "Now he can throw a party for a dozen people who want to feel hip and they can all blow off the tops of their heads. He'll get high for the first or second time in his life and he'll turn some square little chick on for the first time and she'll come across, also for the first time. He's getting his twenty's worth out of the bit."

"Sure."

"Everybody's smoking now," Shank said. "A guy like this one thought he was pretty far out a few years ago when he had a martini on an empty stomach. Now he starts reading and talking to people and he decides that juice isn't far out at all. So he has to reach a little farther."

Joe nodded.

"He'll dig it," Shank went on. "It's a bigger kick than juice. Besides, it's illegal. He can get a year and a day just for holding and he knows it. That makes it more of a kick. He can feel like all the hippies he reads about."

"The gospel according to Saint Jack."

"I'm hip, man. He reads Kerouac and he decides to get remote. You shoulda been there, man. You would've got a kick out of the way he came on. Like it was all something out of a spy movie, you know? Sitting down next to me and talking out of the side of his mouth and all. And he fell over when he saw the pad, like we were living on the other side of the moon and it was heaven on wheels."

"Everybody's smoking it," Joe said. "A year or two and they'll make it legal."

"You kidding."

"Why? They'll have to, with everybody turning on right and left. By the time everybody knows it's harmless and non-habit-forming they won't be able to keep the law on the books. It—"

"You're nuts, man."

Joe looked at him, and Shank went on.

"Things get legal because somebody wants them legal, man. Things don't get legal because somebody doesn't want them legal. You think anybody wants pot legal? You think the Mob wants it legal when they can sell it? You think the liquor lobby wants it legal when nobody would drink juice any more if it was? Hell, you think *I* want it legal? I pull in close to a bill a week selling it, a hundred pennies per keeping squares high. If it's legal they'll sell it in the drugstores, man. Won't that be a bitch?"

Joe nodded, and Shank hauled himself to his feet. "Gotta go," he announced. "You got any idea what time it is?"

"Few minutes after eight."

"That late?"

"Around there."

"Then I better jump."

"What's happening?"

"I got a few things going."

Joe leaned back on the bed and watched Shank go out the door and slam it behind him. The younger boy's footsteps sounded on the stairway, then stopped. The front door banged.

Joe stretched out on the bed, rested his head on the pillow and stared up at the ceiling whose cracked plaster had fallen away in jagged patches. The floor was bare and dirty and the furniture was quietly falling into ruin, the stuffing leaking from the one chair, and broken bedsprings digging down at crazy angles.

Joe alternated between feeling sorry for himself and despising himself, usually was in one mood or the other except for the times a fix lifted him into another mental sphere. In a straight sense, without the realization of marijuana or the stimulation of benzedrine or the sogginess of alcohol or the diffusion of mescalin to eliminate moodiness, he either hated Joe Milani or loathed the world so unnecessarily cruel to him.

You had always been a good enough kid, Joe would tell himself on occasion. Your folks had loved you and you had loved your folks and Rochester hadn't been a bad place to live in. You had run around with a decent bunch of kids and you had done okay in high school and had never gotten into any trouble. Everybody had liked you then. What in the hell had happened to you? Two years in Korea had happened to you, Joe would answer—two years in Korea shooting at people and having the bastards shoot back at you. You had stumbled around, freezing, mud up to your neck and bullets all over the damned place. And then you had had a year in college on the GI bill, the professors throwing things at you that had neither made sense nor mattered a hell of a lot, and there had been nothing to do and no place to go and nobody to be with.

That's what happened to you, Joe would decide. You had been a good kid and they had sent you to Korea to make the world safe for Syngman Rhee, who had been nothing but a fascist bastard to begin with and who was finished now anyway and the Koreans behind half-a-dozen eight balls. They had sent you over there and when they had brought you back there had been nothing stateside for you. Nothing had mattered any more, nothing had fit any more, and when you had gone home to Rochester there had been nobody to talk to. The same people had been there, the same guys—even if they had aged a year or two they had only gotten deader from the neck up. Your folks had been there but it hadn't been the same with them, and the girls had been there and it hadn't been the same with them, either, and all in all Rochester hadn't been worth a damn and New York University had been worth less of a damn and the whole world had gotten dead set on driving you out of your alleged mind.

Sure, Joe thought.

Or, his mood alternating, he would accuse himself: You're just a no-good bastard and you've screwed up everything you've ever touched. Yeah, you had been a happy enough guy in high school. You had never had a thought in your life and you had never done anything except swing bats at baseballs and bang silly little girls in back seats. So you had gone through basic training and had started shaking when they sent live ammo ten feet over your head. So you had shipped to Korea and had aimed your gun at the sky most of the time because you had been too scared to kill anybody. You hadn't had enough guts to have been a conscientious objector or enough guts to have been a soldier—but you had had an anonymous enough body to have been stuck in the middle, a gun in your hand and a hole in your head.

And you had found a woman in Japan, little Michiko, flat-faced Mickey, the sweetest and warmest woman in the world, Mickey of the saffron arms and legs and thighs and breasts and belly, a girl named Mickey who had loved you. And, you gutless no-good wop son of a bitch, you hadn't had the guts to make a Sayonara scene. You had left her there.

Joe Gutless. You had dropped out of NYU because you hadn't been able to knuckle down and study. You had left Rochester because it had been too tough for you to adjust, and you hadn't wanted to do anything unless it was real easy. No guts, no push, no drive, no interest in anything or anybody. You were a faceless wop named Joe Gutless Milani who deserved whatever you got.

And now you did nothing. Now you were Hip or Beat or whatever word they were calling it this month. You had been spending years doing nothing at all. That was the hell of it.

You didn't work. Getting a gig as a messenger boy for a week at a clip wasn't working. Bussing tables at the Automat for a day or two at a time wasn't working. Bumming off Shank, bumming from the women you crawled into an occasional bed with, bumming off anybody who happened to have bread or food or an empty bed or a lonesome gland wasn't working.

You floated.

For the time being you padded down with Shank, as lousy a guy as you were, who pushed pot in an extremely small-time way, who carried a knife and would one day or another stick somebody with it if he hadn't already.

You floated. You pushed pot and chewed peyote.

You drifted. You were impotent with half the women you slept with and you didn't muscle much of a kick out of the other half.

You stank.

Joe rolled off the bed and eased himself into the chair. Since the joint of marijuana was still in his pocket, he thought for a moment about smoking it, but then decided to hold on to it for a while. Next morning would be time enough. He would wake up and reach for the little cylinder of pot and blow off the top of his head before he opened his eyes—that would be nice. Instead of the joint he fished a regular cigarette from his other pocket and lit it.

He drew smoke into his lungs, thinking it would be much more satisfying to draw another kind of smoke into his lungs, and wondering how long it would be before he started playing interesting games with a needle. Not that pot led you to the hard stuff, it didn't. It was just that eventually you yourself would wind up trying the hard stuff even if most pot smokers never did. You, Joe Milani, would, because it was there for you and it was a new kick and there were not nearly enough kicks in the world.

He blew out the smoke and took another drag on the cigarette, a longer drag that burned up maybe a third of the cigarette in one long pull, and he coughed on the cloud of smoke.

Joe closed his eyes.

Anita Carbone. Right now he couldn't be sure if he hated the world, or Joe Milani, or both; but one thing he was relatively certain of: if it weren't for the fundamental inadequacies in Joe Milani, or the world, or both, Joe Milani and Anita Carbone might have a future of some sort. Maybe not a white-gown-and-wedding-bells-and-rice type of scene, but a future one way or the other.

Because Anita, by all the rules, answered to the perfect girl. She was a good girl, Joe knew, an Italian girl, and a virgin who obviously didn't owe her virginity to the fact nobody had bothered to ask her. A bright girl, too, her intelligence compounded of Harlem intuition and Hunter education. She was damned attractive physically, he told himself, and damned pleasant company. Clean and fresh without being so square the two of you couldn't talk to each other. Although he had been high when he had picked her up, and had been deeply attracted to her then, he had liked her even more, later, as a low had started to come on.

It was a shame he would never see her again.

The part of him that hated Joe Milani said: *What does a chick like that need with a bastard like you? What are you going to do for her: turn her on? take her to bed? drive her as nutty as you are?*

The part of Joe Milani that hated the world said:

She's just not your type of chick, man. She's just not for you, and she's never gonna be, no matter what you try to do about it. The two of you are living in different worlds, and if you think it was a long way from Japan to the States, it's miles more from Hip to Square.

And Joe Milani listened to both voices, listened to them with both ears, and decided that both voices were entirely correct.

So why see her again, he asked himself. And why make a pass at her when the result had to be one of two things—either she would throw the pass right back in your face, or the pair of you would wind up in bed. Both eventualities, in the final analysis, would be equally unpleasant.

Damn, it was wrong! Joe cursed silently. You were supposed to go to high school and then college, the army cutting in before or after. Then you married a good Italian girl and settled down and bought one of those new houses in the suburbs and snagged a job with your old man or sold insurance or found something else you didn't have to kill yourself doing and at which you could make a fairly decent living. That was what you were supposed to do.

But what you were supposed to do was also impossible, inconceivable, and couldn't work out no matter how much grass you smoked. You couldn't go back again, that was the hell of it. Squares could turn Hip if they were sick enough, but Hips like you, Joe Milani, couldn't seem to return to Squaresville.

It would be so nice to be square, Joe thought. That was something the squares never got into their heads, that their world was a far more attractive one when you were sitting on the other side of the fence. Was the grass always greener?

Well, no. Because sometimes grass turned brown, especially that Mexican brown that smelled a little different and seemed a little stronger. The joint in his pockets was half regular green and half Mexican brown and it was a good thick bomber, and he fingered it lovingly, his fingers cool and expectant on the brown wheat-straw paper.

No. Joe rejected the temptation.

Not tonight. Tomorrow, he promised himself, but not tonight.

He stood up, wanting a woman suddenly, wanting a woman but not wanting the woman he had just left, the woman he could never possibly make it with. The image in his mind was simply Woman. He paced the room and thought for a minute and decided the right woman for the moment would be Fran, good old Fran, sick little Fran who lived a few blocks away and always had room in her bed for him. She would probably want to get a little high first on something or other, but that was all right when you stopped to think about it.

Why not get high?

Why not ball with Fran? Joe Milani poked at the question.

Why not, indeed?

He left the apartment and hurried down the stairs, head high and arms swinging at his sides. It was cool outside, the sky dark, the streetlights lit.

He walked easily, west on Saint Marks to Third Avenue, down Third to Fran's big and wonderful pad, a third-floor loft on Cooper Square.

He didn't ring the bell because none existed, and if there had been one he would not have bothered to ring. At Fran's place you opened that always unlocked outer door and climbed those grim, unlighted stairs until you reached Fran's door where you knocked just in case some stud was ahead of you.

Joe paused at the door, undecided whether to knock or to turn around, head down the stairs and out of the building, up Third to Saint Marks and over Saint Marks to his own place—saying to hell with Fran and to hell with Joe Milani and to hell, for that matter, with just about everybody.

He knocked at the door.

Fran Paine answered the door. She was alone, her badly bleached blonde hair hanging down to her waist, her breasts huge in the man's white dress shirt ill-designed for chests such as hers—alone in a hovel where books, bottles and butts littered the floor.

Fran closed the door behind him and the two sat down on a broken-up couch. They each drank a bottle of cherry-flavored cough syrup containing 2 minims of chloroform and 43 milligrams of codeine, mixed with extracts of squill, ipecac and sanguinaria.

The cough syrup was sweet, a little too sweet. But in a short time it had been consumed and they had their high—not the screamily floating high of pot or the pounding, pacing, madcap high of pep pills, but a soft and gently drowsy and beneficent high, the high of codeine, an opium derivative, that made everything much easier to bear.

Joe took off the man's white dress shirt, wondering vaguely but without concern what guy had left the shirt at Fran's pad, the last stud to share Fran's big double bed.

He took off Fran's skirt. She wore nothing under the skirt or shirt—she rarely did, complaining that underwear inhibited her.

He removed his own clothes.

Their love-making came down as a long stretch. Opiates such as codeine serve only to lessen a woman's inhibitions; in a man they encourage impotence. But after a while Joe's need for love, combined with the insistence of Fran's practiced hands and the attraction of Fran's equally practiced body, clutched them together like two hungry, homeless children who strained desperately to find something.

Something long lost.

Afterward, as they were falling asleep, the codeine swiftly bringing on unconsciousness, Joe heard voices, loud and frighteningly real, screaming in his brain. But, finally, he slept, his eyes shut against the world and his face pressed into a pillow. And he dreamed there was blood in the back of his throat, and that he couldn't cough it out.

When the sun hit Joe in the eyes, his hand began to move. The fingers uncoiled, crept along the edge of the bed, reaching across the table at the side. The fingers fumbled at the clutter on the top of the table—hairpins, curlers, small bottles of cosmetics, the foil wrapper from a prophylactic. The fingers then curled around a pack of cigarettes and shook the pack until one cigarette popped out. Then, the cigarette held loosely between the second and third fingers, the hand returned to the bed.

Cigarette between lips. Hand back to table. Matches.

Eyes open, you scratch a match against the striking surface of the matchbook, bring the flame to the end of the cigarette, drag on the cigarette, shake out the match and flip it onto the floor.

You sit up, take another drag on the cigarette. The smoke's in your lungs, and then you take a breath.

Joe Milani was awake.

He got up from the bed, balancing the cigarette on the edge of the table, and groped around for clothing. Fran was up and gone but his clothes were still on the floor. His clothes were dirty and clung to his body like old friends when he put them on.

Dressed, he reclaimed his cigarette before it could add another burn to the row at the table edge. Walking to the window, he opened it to get a breath of fresh air and find out the time. The sun, still fairly low in the sky, indicated it was about ten-thirty.

Fran had left no note; not particularly surprising. Joe rummaged through the refrigerator and salvaged some milk and the end of a salami. He drank the milk in one swallow and gnawed at the salami, hard and salty, but tasty, so he ate it all.

He left Fran's place. On the street he felt lost at first, unsure of where to go, not wanting anything and a little off-balance. His feet headed toward his own room but stopped as he realized it was pointless to go home—Shank had probably left by now and Joe had no desire to see Shank, anyway.

Then Milani remembered the marijuana.

His hand dug at once into his pocket. There was a scrap of paper there and a pack of regular cigarettes, and at first he thought that the joint had disappeared, maybe Fran had taken it or he himself had gone and lost it somewhere. Then, when he found it at the bottom of the pocket, his fingers examined it without removing it. It seemed to be all right and he relaxed.

Joe wandered aimlessly around the East Side, then headed west on Fourth Street. A dollar bill was wrapped around some loose change in one pocket and he thought about getting something to eat but nothing appealed. He passed a delicatessen selling loaves of French bread for fifteen cents and he stood on the sidewalk practically five minutes, unable to decide whether or not to buy a loaf. Finally he decided no and walked on.

Immobility.

He recognized it now, felt it in his bones and skin, felt it creeping up on him and infecting him with a paralysis peculiarly his own, a paralysis the rest of the world never shared with him. It was his, his paralysis, his immobility—his alone, and when it came he could only sit and ponder it or walk and ponder it or lie down and ponder it, because there was absolutely nothing else in the world he could do or want to do.

Immobility.

At Washington Square he stared at the statue of Garibaldi, his hand on his sword, and Joe remembered the legend at NYU—a legend which, in one form or another, seemed prevalent on every campus in the world. When Garibaldi drew his sword, the legend said, that meant a virgin had walked by.

As Joe stood contemplating the statue of Garibaldi he decided the legend was all wrong. The old soldier wouldn't draw that damned sword of his if all the virgins in the western world paraded in front of him. The old wop was made out of stone and he would stand for the rest of eternity with his hand on his sword and his eyes staring ahead vacantly.

In that particular respect, Joe decided, the old wop and the young wop had a lot in common.

Sitting hunched on a bench in the park, Joe pulled out his cigarettes and lit one. After the first puff he let

the cigarette remain between his fingers, his eyes on
the column of smoke rising perhaps two or three
inches into the air before the wind blew it away. When
the cigarette burned all the way down he let it drop
from his fingers to the asphalt where it continued to
burn. It went out before it could burn to the end.

He lit another cigarette.

Immobility.

The Good Humor Man passed, his wagon full of
ice cream. Maybe an ice cream would taste good, Joe
mused.

Then again maybe it wouldn't.

Go to hell, Good Humor Man.

*Very few things matter and nothing matters very
much.* Where had Joe heard that? It didn't sound like a
quote, and yet it had a very familiar ring. Where had
he seen it?

It didn't matter, he decided. Of course it didn't
matter. That was the whole point of it, anyway.

Immobility.

It was a very beat condition, this immobility, and he
found himself wondering why nobody had bothered to
describe it in a novel. The beat writers were uniformly
lousy, but one of them nevertheless should have managed to get hipped on the notion of transferring that
marvelous state of nothingness to paper. Or was the
condition unique with Joe? The human condition, the
beat condition, the stony stonelike condition.

Immobility.

It wasn't the same as sitting with nothing to do, Joe pondered. There were any number of things he could do, any number of people he could hunt up. He could find a woman or find a friend or run up to Times Square and see a movie or get a hotdog at Grant's or sit over coffee at Bickford's or make the coffee-house scene at The Palermo or one of the other spots. Or he could buzz up to the library and bury himself in a book or head back to his place and read something or write something or smoke the stick in his pocket.

There were many things to do. A veritable myriad of possibilities.

None of which attracted him.

Back to immobility, he told himself. Let's analyze this. Let's take it apart and see what's running around inside. Let's figure out how it's put together. Let's peel off the outer wrapper and dig inside it once and for all and figure out why in the hell we are sitting on a bench in Washington Square Park with a cigarette burning to hell and gone between our tobacco-stained fingers with nothing to do and no place to go and the world whirling around and making absolutely no sense at all.

Let's nail it to the floor and throw darts at it. Let's jump up and down on it and pick the meat off its bones.

Let's do something, for Christ's sake.

Your name had been Joe Milani, then as now, and you had been taking courses at NYU and living in a ratty room on West 12th Street. You had had a landlady whose false teeth had been so perfect they had resembled false teeth, and the room had always been neat as a pin because the landlady habitually cleaned it up and hung up your clothes after you had thrown them on the floor, and had swept up your cigarettes when you had stamped them out on the linoleum. And you had been taking a bevy of courses, exams coming up in a week—not finals, just midterms, and you had been smart enough so the exams had looked to be a breeze.

You had come home from school one day. You had sat down in front of the table, the room's excuse for a desk, and you had propped up a book. You had been taking a course in the development of the early English novel and the book in front of you had been *Humphrey Clinker* by one Tobias Smollett. You had had to get the book read so you had flipped it open to page one and had started reading.

That had been at three-thirty.

At four o'clock you had gotten to page forty-five because you could read like a bat out of hell, except not like a blind bat out of hell because blind bats obviously couldn't read. Did they have braille books for blind bats, Joe wondered momentarily. It was worth thinking about, but forget it for now. You're contemplating immobility, remember?

So at four o'clock you had been on page forty-five and you had kept on reading.

At five o'clock you had been on page forty-five.

At six-thirty you had been on page forty-five.

You hadn't taken your eyes off that page. You hadn't moved from that hard wooden chair.

But you had still been on page forty-five. Seven more butts had littered the linoleum and your beard had grown perceptibly longer than when you had started, but that's all that had happened.

You had still been on page forty-five.

Three days later you had still been on page forty-five. You had eaten eight or nine meals, had gone to The Palermo once or twice, had talked very briefly with the landlady when she had entered to make the bed. But you hadn't managed to read any more or do anything except smoke a number of packs of cigarettes and drop three days out of your life. You hadn't gone to classes or read anything else, and never in your life would you progress further than page forty-five in *Humphrey Clinker*.

By one Tobias Smollett.

Joe dropped the cigarette, squashed it with his foot, lit another and closed his eyes when the end-smoke from the cigarette hit them and burned them a little. Then he opened his eyes, dragged on the cigarette, blew out smoke and let his eyelids drop shut again.

Now why had page forty-five stopped him so cold?

All right. To begin with, *Humphrey Clinker* by Tobias Smollett had been a grade-A bore. The whole course, from *Pamela* to *Mansfield Park*, had been a grade-A bore. The whole bit at NYU, from the required geology course he hadn't wanted to take to the advanced English courses he had looked forward to with a great deal of pleasure—all had added up to a grade-A bore.

So he had been bored then as now. Was that any reason to spend half his life on page forty-five?

It wasn't.

And if he were bored, didn't it figure he should do something to stop being bored?

It did.

Then what the hell.

Immobility, you damned fool.

Joe dropped the cigarette before he was finished with it. The cigarette fell from its perch between his fingers and dropped to the pavement. It rolled several feet into the middle of the walk and a passer-by stepped on it without noticing it.

He had dropped the cigarette because he had just come upon a great eternal truth, and the shock of discovery had been too much for him.

Immobility was the opposite of something!

The opposite of mobility, obviously. But as Joe looked at immobility from that unique point of view, some things began to make sense.

Sitting on a bench like an oyster on the floor of the Atlantic was the same at the root as running around and turning on and banging good old Fran and drinking too much and raising all kinds of quiet hell.

The same thing in reverse.

The reaction.

The other side of the coin, the other face of the Roman gatekeeper, the opposite.

Ah!

Because, Joe thought, when you did move you moved at the speed of light. You could do everything at once, go every place and know everybody and read a book in an hour and do all your work at school with both eyes shut and race around madly and dig everything. When you were immobile, nothing appealed; when you were—well, call it mobile for the time being —when you were mobile you could dig everything because everything was dynamically real and vivid and alive and breathing and gasping with things that mattered.

Ergo: the running and the joy-jumping and all was the same as the sitting and walking and lying down. Ergo: immobility was not a phenomenon but a result of whatever made him the person he was, the Joe Milani who lived on Saint Marks Place and sat on benches in Washington Square.

Which raised another inevitably interesting question.

Why?

It was an interesting question. Joe reflected on it for several hours, conjuring up all sorts of interesting notions without getting any place in particular. The hell of it was that he had been over it all before without getting anywhere then either, and he was beginning to develop the sneaking suspicion that the pondering and contemplating was not an entity in itself but another facet of the condition, the mass neurosis of the Hip and the individual neurosis of the person named Joe Milani. He might have followed this last train of thought a little further except that somebody coughed, somebody close to him, and his eyes left the spot between the second and third fingers of his right hand and looked upward.

Into the eyes of Anita Carbone.

4

Shank was being followed. Shank heard the pattern of footsteps behind him and saw the familiar figure visible again and then again over his left shoulder. Shank's first reactions were automatic. He stopped abruptly, wheeled, headed across the street and doubled back along the block. As Shank turned he spotted a man wearing a grey overcoat and a droopy felt hat shading the face—the latter dodge not enough to arouse suspicions, but enough to conceal the man's features adequately.

The tail was sharp. He continued walking in the same direction about ten paces before he turned and began following Shank once more.

All right. Shank had a tail. Now he had to keep the tail from realizing that his presence had been detected. If the tail knew Shank were on to him, the whole game would become that much harder. Shank had not decided whether to shake the tail or lead him to the upper reaches of the Bronx; in either case, it would be best to keep the tail in the dark.

Shank stepped inside the first corner drugstore and moved to the counter to buy cigarettes. Evidently the tail had not yet caught on because Shank could see him through the window as he—Shank—bent down to pick up a coin he managed to drop. Shank also ascertained he had never seen the tail before.

After lighting a cigarette to make his purchase seem a natural one, Shank left the store and ambled down the street as he thought about the tail. He wondered where the guy had picked him up. Shank had quit the BMT at Union Square. The drugstore was at Broadway and Tenth. This meant the tail had been with him all the way from the meet with Mau-Mau or had just picked him up on the street.

Shank tended to reject the second possibility. He rarely rode the BMT from Times Square, rarely got off at 14th Street, rarely walked along Broadway. The first possibility struck him as being much more likely. Could the guy have been with him on the subway? It was possible. And if he had been, and if he had seen the meet with Mau-Mau and knew what was happening, there might be trouble. A lot of trouble.

The Mau-Mau was a middleman, a sort of wholesaler. Most of the marijuana smoked in the United States was raised in Mexico and smuggled across the border. If the shipment were part of a syndicate operation, nobody needed the Mau-Mau. If, on the other hand, the guy who brought it in were a freelance hauling across a pound or two at a time, the Mau-Mau operated. He bought it by the pound and sold it by the ounce to the small pushers, and he profited enough at this to keep up one of the posh pads in one of the posh sections of Harlem.

About an hour ago the Mau-Mau had laid three ounces of very choice merchandise on Shank in exchange for twenty-five dollars. The three ounces nestled in a small, brown envelope in Shank's back pocket.

Which meant that Shank was hotter than a rat in a smoky sewer.

Shank took a right turn at First Avenue and headed down in the general direction of his room. Stalling for time, he stopped at a candy store on First between Ninth and Tenth, took a seat at the counter and ordered a chocolate egg cream. He had to think through this situation.

The tail, whoever he was, had not tried to bust Shank while he had been with the Mau-Mau. Maybe the Mau-Mau had the tail bought and the guy was trying to make his quota on small pushers. Maybe the guy was afraid to make a pinch in Harlem. Maybe, for that matter, the guy figured Shank had a heavier bundle at his pad, in which case the tail probably had not the slightest idea of where Shank lived, which was fine with Shank. If his pad had been known the fuzz would have arrested him on the street and would have had somebody else bust the pad. But this wasn't the way the game was being played.

Shank sipped at the egg cream and wished he had ordered something more drinkable. He thought of leaving the thing unfinished but passed up the idea because he had to appear straight all the way.

Suppose, Shank thought, he didn't go back to the

pad? That would prevent the joker from finding out Shank's address, but it would also practically invite an arrest. And Shank was holding three big ounces.

Suppose he shook the tail? That wouldn't be too hard to do, not with the joker shadowing him on foot. Just take a corner fast and hop into a cab and goodbye, tail. But there were two things wrong with such a course of action. For one thing, suppose this were a double-shadow job—Shank losing one man only to have the other stick with him, which would mean the end of the ball game. Or suppose Shank would make it clean?—then the guy would be after Shank for the rest of his life. Would that be good?

No—the best move would be to lead the tail right back to the room. There was less than an ounce in the room, anyway, and the most Shank could get for that would be a year and a day. There were two raps for possession of marijuana—straight possession of any amount, and possession with intent to sell. Just holding was a misdemeanor, but if you held enough so that they could call it possession with intent you caught a felony rap.

Under an ounce was definitely just holding, pure and simple. But how about three ounces? That might go either way. Shank was not sure.

He finished the egg cream and sauntered out of the candy store, his mind made up. He had to head straight for his pad and get rid of the stuff in his pocket before he was in the door. If he could ditch the rest, fine. If not—well it was a year and a day, and for a first offense he might get off with a suspended sentence. This was the safest way to play it.

He saw the tail over his left shoulder when he went out the door. Shank strode down First to Saint Marks, pacing at his usual speed. He turned at the corner, spotting the tail again as he did so, and headed toward his own building.

Now how in hell was he going to ditch the stuff? Three ounces was three ounces—a hell of a lot to chuck in the river. The stuff around his pad was nothing, less than an ounce and not the best stuff in the world, anyway. But what he had in his pocket was top-grade and he was looking forward to a stick or two himself. He had twenty-five dollars invested in it, and by the time he had it softened a little with Bull Durham he would have close to a bill's worth right there. Sixty bucks if he sold it by the ounce, but a bill easy if you figured the guys who bought a stick or two at a buck a stick.

And who in the hell wanted to throw away a bill, Shank thought savagely.

He stopped and pulled out the pack of cigarettes. His own building was just three doors away now and he had not managed to solve everything to his satisfaction. Suppose—Shank sweated to concentrate— suppose he planted the stuff somewhere inside the building but not inside the apartment? That way it probably wouldn't be found, and if it were they would have a rough time pinning it to him.

But where would he stash it so the guy would miss it and nobody else would walk off with it? It would be one hell of a joke if Shank could manage to keep it from the cop only to have one of the local yokels wind up with it.

When he reached the door he decided he had to find out how far back the tail was hanging. He chanced a quick glance around and spotted him a few doors down the street. That gave Shank plenty of room if he played it right.

He opened the door and went inside. He glanced around the vestibule but it never had looked barer than it did just then. Where the hell…?

It seemed obvious when he saw it. Shank walked to the mailboxes and dropped the envelope of marijuana into a slot marked MRS. HERMAN RODJINCKSZI, praying silently that Mrs. Herman Rodjinckszi would stay away from her mailbox for the next couple of hours.

Then he took the stairs two at a time, wondering how long the tail would stay on the street before he decided to have a look inside. He got his answer while he was opening his own door, when he heard the downstairs door open.

He closed the door, sliding the bolt into place. Then he raced around the apartment, grabbing the half-empty brown envelope from the table, snatching up the packet of cigarette papers although there was nothing illegal about owning them, picking up also the sack of Bull Durham on the off chance some pot was mixed in with the tobacco. He hadn't remembered spicing up that particular sack but there was no point taking chances.

The toilet worked on the first flush for the first time in a good three weeks. He flushed it again for the sheer hell of it and let himself relax completely for the first time since he had spotted the tail.

The relaxation did not last. Suppose Joe had left the stick some place around? Suppose there was a roach on the floor somewhere? Christ, all the cops needed was a grain of the stuff and they could stick you with possession if they wanted you badly enough. Suppose the son of a—

A knock sounded at the door.

He took a quick look around. He glanced under the bed, finding nothing.

"Open up there. Police."

Police—well, that wasn't much of a surprise, Shank chuckled to himself. He opened the door.

Close up, the tail seemed meek and unimpressive. He could have been sitting across from Shank in the subway all the way from 125th Street without Shank having been aware of him. But the man's eyes indicated toughness and capability.

"Want to let me in?" the tail said.

"Want to show me your credentials?"

The man was Detective First Grade Peter J. Samuelson, Narcotics Bureau. Which, come to think of it—Shank gave a mental shrug—wasn't much of a surprise either.

"C'mon inside," he said.

Detective Samuelson went through the motions then, but it was obvious he no longer expected to discover anything. The first look at Shank's face had told him the place was clean. Samuelson bothered with a search only on the off chance he might strike uranium. He made Shank stand with his hands on the wall while he went through his pockets. All he found were two opened packs of cigarettes, a wallet with a few dollars and some uninteresting cards, and the knife.

"You expecting trouble?" the detective inquired.

Shank gave no reply.

"There's a law against knives like this," the detective pointed out softly. "Can't buy 'em, can't sell 'em, can't own 'em. I could haul you in on this and let you cool off in the Tombs."

"That what they got you boys doing? Looking around for switchblades?"

And now the cop said nothing.

"You pick four kids off the street," Shank delivered the brief lecture. "Pick up any four kids and three of them got knives like that one. Bigger, most of them."

The cop laughed, unpleasantly. He pressed the button and the blade of the knife shot out. The cop looked at the knife for several seconds, closed it and dropped it into Shank's pocket.

"Here," he said, "keep your toy."

Shank fell silent.

The cop went ahead and checked the room. He knew all the right places—the toilet tank, the window sill, under the mattress, inside the shoes by the bed. Shank wore a pair of desert boots and the cop double-checked them because there was enough room in the toe to hold illegal merchandise.

The cop combed just about everything, and while he did he cursed softly to himself because he knew that the search would do no good. Somehow or other Shank had tumbled to him and ditched the stuff, and it was a cinch it was nowhere around the apartment.

Well, it served Detective Samuelson right. He knew he should have collared the little bastard on the street instead of taking chances. Next time he would know better.

"Okay," Samuelson said, finally. "I guess you're clean."

Shank smiled.

"When did you make me?" the detective asked casually.

Shank shrugged. His eyes said he could not possibly be familiar with what the cop was talking about but the cop knew better.

"When you turned around," the cop said, reflecting aloud. "Sure. You already had cigarettes. I should have known—I saw you with one before you got on the subway. And you didn't throw away an empty pack. I should have picked you up the minute you walked into the drugstore."

Shank smiled again.

"I was working close," the cop said, rubbing his nose ruefully. "I should have figured on you spotting me but I thought I was clear. How did you happen to notice me?"

"You were lousy," Shank summed it up.

For a minute the cop looked as though he were ready to explode. Then his features relaxed.

"You won this round," he said. "How many more do you think you'll win?"

"I don't know what you're talking about."

"The hell you don't. You'll know what I'm talking about when we get you, punk, and don't think we're not going to get you sooner or later. You were clean until today. We didn't know you were alive. Now we know and we won't forget until we nail the lid on."

Shank kept silent.

"Sooner or later you'll be holding and we'll be on to you. Sooner or later you'll slip and we'll grab you. We'll watch you so hard you won't be able to hit the toilet without looking over your shoulder to see who's there."

"Yeah?"

"Yeah," the cop said.

"You try to watch every guy who's selling and you'll

need more men than you got on the whole force. You got any idea how many guys are selling?"

"A fair idea."

"Lots of them, aren't there?"

"Too many."

"Well, how are you gonna—"

"We won't watch 'em all," the cop said. "Just the ones we know about. And we know about you."

Shank said nothing for a moment. He was enjoying the conversation but at the same time he was annoyed the cops were on to him.

"What the hell," Shank said. "I don't know what you're so burned about. I wasn't holding anyway."

The cop laughed again.

"I wasn't," Shank defended himself. "I—"

"You took a good three ounces off the Mau-Mau," the cop said. "Probably more. And in case you're wondering, we busted the Mau-Mau just after you left. It's the third time for him, the third intent rap, and this means the Mau-Mau has a home for the rest of his life as a guest of the United States Government. You might want to think about that for a while."

The cop left.

Two hours later Shank smashed Mrs. Herman Rodjinckszi's mailbox with a hammer and reclaimed the envelope.

5

The Hoi Polloi is a small Chinese restaurant one flight above the street on Eighth Street off Sixth Avenue. Anita Carbone had never been there before, but now she was eating pork with Chinese vegetables. Although the food was good, its taste was lost on her. Something very strange was happening to her and she was doing her best to keep up with it, to figure out what was going on.

Joe Milani sat opposite Anita and filled his mouth with chicken chow mein, washing it down with tea. Soon, she knew, the meal would be finished and the waiter would present her with the check. And she would pay it.

She had never bought dinner for a boy before. When she went out to dinner with a date, he paid for the meal. No young man had ever so much as asked her to pay her own way, let alone to swing the entire check.

But this was different, Anita felt. She had picked up Joe Milani all by herself. He had been sitting alone, and she had found him, and otherwise they would never have been sitting at the same table in the Hoi Polloi.

Of course, she argued with herself, she hadn't exactly picked him up. She had gone to the Village again, admittedly, but not for the purpose of meeting Joe. He had been on her mind, of course. He had been rather interesting in The Palermo, naturally, and certainly not the type of fellow she had been used to—nothing run-of-the-mill about Joe Milani. But she hadn't been consciously scouting him when she had wandered through Washington Square. Not really.

When she had seen him there, it had been only natural for her to stop and say hello. It would have been rude to walk right by him without a word.

So when you looked at it that way…Anita's thoughts trailed off.

"Two cents," Joe said.

She glanced up, startled.

"For your thoughts," he explained. "You look real deep. Buried in thought. Wouldn't be fair to offer you a penny for your thoughts, not when they're so profound. So I'll make it two cents."

Anita smiled.

"What are you thinking about? Tell me."

"Nothing," she said. "I don't know. Just thinking."

He waited.

"Emptiness," she said. "You know how somebody says his mind is a blank? Not like that exactly. Not that my mind is blank, but what I'm thinking about…well, everything. And everything I'm thinking about is blank."

Joe offered her a cigarette and she took it, put it between her lips and lit it. She thought that she could smoke in the restaurant, that it was all right, but that she should remember not to smoke outside on the street because her grandmother would be mad at her. She thought how funny her grandmother was about things like that and she wanted to laugh but didn't. She remembered when Joe had offered her a cigarette in the park, and she had explained that it wasn't right to smoke in the street if you were a girl.

Depends what you smoke, he had said. And she had laughed, a little uncertainly, and then later on he had mentioned pot and she had remembered the marijuana smokers in her own neighborhood, the marijuana smokers and the heroin users. Her disapproval had shown at the time and he had laughed at her, telling her that marijuana was not bad for you at all, that a New York Public Health Report had certified it as harmless, that it wouldn't hurt you a bit. She had not been sure whether she should believe him or no.

"Emptiness," he repeated, waking her up again. And she nodded slowly and focused on the tip of her cigarette. It was glowing dully.

"It's all set up," she said. "All patterned out. My whole life, practically. I live with my grandmother. She's a nice old lady. And she keeps the place looking good, Joe. It's supposed to be a slum—you know, East Harlem, a slum, it says so in the paper. But our apartment—I've seen worse, believe me."

He nodded. She closed her eyes for a moment and pictured the apartment, her grandmother curled up in the cane-bottom rocker, rocking slowly, shriveled, small. Anita opened her eyes.

"I go to Hunter," she said. "If you come from New York and you do well in high school you go to college for free. I did well in high school, Joe. They told me I was very bright. So I went to Hunter. You know what I'm majoring in?"

"You told me," he said. "History, isn't it?"

"Government—not very different, really. It's sort of interesting some of the time. The courses."

Joe nodded and thought about Smollett.

"And I go out on dates," she went on. "I'm not a wallflower. I've even got a steady boyfriend. Isn't that a stupid word? Boyfriend. He's a friend and he's a boy. His name is Ray. Ray Rico. He's good-looking and he's smart. Goes to Cooper Union, studying to be an engineer. You've got to be a whip to get into Cooper Union. He'll walk out of that school and walk into a job with IBM or somebody at ten thousand dollars a year. You know how much that is? Two hundred dollars a week. That's a lot of money. And the more he works for them the more money he makes. He told me he ought to be able to go as high as twenty-five thousand. You know what's funny? When you don't make much money it's so much a week. A steno makes sixty-five a week, not three thousand and something a year. Nobody makes four hundred a week. You don't think about it that way. It's funny, I guess."

Joe smiled. "I worked in a drugstore once," he said. "I made seventy-five cents an hour. While I was in high school. Deliveries, dusting the stock, sweeping the floor. That type of scene. You ever hear anybody talk about making twenty bucks an hour?"

But Anita's eyes were staring into the far-away. What was she looking at, Joe wondered. Emptiness, perhaps. Space.

"All in a pattern," she said. "When Ray graduated from high school he knew what kind of a job he would finally have. Now he knows he'll marry me. We go out once, twice a week. A movie, a cup of coffee. At first he kissed me once at the door every night before I went inside. On the mouth. Now we sit on the roof once in a while and he touches my breasts. That sounds funny, doesn't it? But that's what he does. He touches my breasts. I guess pretty soon he'll start putting his hand under my skirt. Then when there's nothing else to do but go to bed—we'll be married. And he'll graduate and get his good job and we'll buy a little house on the Island. A split-level. I've seen pictures of them. Small and ugly but very chic, *very* modern."

She closed her eyes and saw the pictures of the split-levels. She remembered wondering why anybody would want to live in one of them.

"I'll have an electric kitchen," she said. "Electric range and electric refrigerator and electric dishwasher and electric frying pan and electric coffee maker and an electric sink. They'll probably have electric sinks by then. They've got everything else. And we'll have two-point-three children and one of them will have to be a boy and one a girl and God knows what the fraction will be. And we'll have a big television set and we'll sit in front of it every night. All of us. All four-point-three of us. We'll stare at that screen and let it think for us nice and electrically. Real togetherness. We wouldn't watch television alone. It wouldn't be right. Do things in a group. The family that prays together stays together."

"You make it sound pretty sad," Joe ventured.

She looked hard at him. "That's just it," she said. "I make it sound terrible. And, you know, it is not that terrible. Not for most people. They would tell me I'm insane to make such a fuss. Look at me, I've got a nice guy, he'll make money, we'll have a good life. It's nice. Isn't that a great word? Nice. And it fits. It's nice. For everybody else in the world it's nice and I don't want it."

"What do you want?"

"I don't know."

"Don't you?"

Anita put out her cigarette. "I don't know," she said. "I don't know anything. I think I'm cracking up. Can you believe that? I think I'm cracking up. A nice intelligent nice Italian nice bright nice nice nice girl and I'm positively cracking up. Let's get out of here, Joe."

She glanced at the check for the first time—no more than a dollar-seventy. She was pleasantly surprised. She put two dollars on the table and they walked out. They walked over Eighth Street to Macdougal to the park and found a bench to sit on. On the way she didn't know whether to take his arm or no.

They sat on the bench and were silent. She observed the passers-by and she wondered who she was. She had to be somebody. She watched boys, men with beards, girls with very long and very wild hair, and she wondered if she were one of them. She thought about the girls and boys in her classes at Hunter, the other girls and boys in her neighborhood, and she wondered if she were like them. She had to be like somebody. You couldn't be all by yourself, she thought. You would go crazy that way.

"I talked a blue streak," Anita said. "Before. In the restaurant. I really went on. I ran off at the mouth."

"You had things to say."

"I never said them before. I hardly thought them."

"But they were still there."

"But I hardly even thought them," she said. "I could never tell them to anybody. Not to Ray. If I tried, he would look at me as though I were insane. And I met you for the second time and I can tell you everything."

"Maybe it's because you don't know me."

"Or because I do."

Joe lit a cigarette and gave one to Anita who took it without hesitation, smoking it for the first time without the persistent sensation of there being something inherently wrong with the act.

"What do you do, Joe?"

"Not much."

"I don't mean for a living. I mean what do you do? You know what I mean."

He shrugged. "I live with another guy. I mentioned him. Shank. The guy I was with at The Palermo."

She nodded.

"You sure you want to know all this? Some of it isn't pretty. You may want to go away from me. You may not like me as much any more," Joe said carefully.

"I want to hear."

"He sells marijuana," he said. "He makes a living. He pays the rent, slips me a buck now and then. He supports me, you could say. I don't cost much. Food, rent, a buck now and then to ball with. Nothing much else."

"He's a…pusher?"

"Not a pusher. He buys and sells. You could call him a connection, sort of. Strictly small-time. He makes enough money so that we live. Not in style but we live."

Anita thought about that. Joe lived because Shank was willing to support him for reasons of his own. By all rules Joe was something contemptible—low, cheap, worthless. But for some reason this did not bother the girl. She judged it unimportant, his earning a living or no.

She felt comfortable with Joe. She could relax with him, a far more important consideration to her.

"So I bum around," he went on. "With Shank, with other people, by myself. I wander. I look at things. That's about it, I guess. I smoke a stick here and there, lie around the pad, sit in the park. I'm a waste of time."

"Could I live with you?"

The question startled her at least as much as it startled him. She hadn't planned on saying that. She hadn't even realized it had been on her mind. But it was out now, in the open, and he was staring at her.

"You don't mean that, Anita."

"Don't I?"

"No. Maybe I made it look like a picnic. You don't understand. It's no picnic. It's a drag, actually. When all is said and done it's a drag. You come on about split-levels and fractional children and you miss making a lot of important connections. You're hipped on forests so much you forget how much you hate trees."

"I don't understand."

"That's where it's at. You don't understand at all. You think this is roses or something. No worries, no sweat. Just dig everything because it's real. You missed a few changes, Anita. You think I'm here because I love it so damn much. That's not it."

"I know."

"Sure you do. You think it's a perfect scene. You think it's free and romantic and wonderful and anybody who works for a living is out of his head. You think you can beat the world by making a scene like this."

"I didn't say that."

He ignored her. "You just don't understand," Joe said. "You think I make the let's-be-beat scene because I like it. I don't. I don't like it at all."

"Then—"

"I make it because there's no other scene I could make. I make it because everything else is just a little bit worse. Not for the world. For me. Personally. It's not the world's fault. It's my fault and I'm stuck with it."

"I know," she said. And when he tried to interrupt her she shook her head. "I understand," she went on. "But you don't. You think you're the only person who thinks your way. Maybe I can't…can't make it…either. I don't know the words yet. I don't know how to talk the way you talk. Just how to think and even that I'm just learning. I don't know who I am. But I know who I'm not. There's a difference. And that's why I want to come and live with you. Why I still want to. Unless you don't want me."

She felt his hand on her arm. She closed her eyes and stopped talking.

"You don't love me, Anita."

"Of course not!"

"Then—"

"I don't love Ray, either. But I could marry him, still without loving him, and the whole world would throw rice at us. Does that make so much more sense?"

"Maybe not."

"Then why can't I live with you?"

He smiled gently. "Your grandmother won't like it," he said. "Even with a nice Italian boy like me. She won't like it at all."

"I'll tell her I'm taking an apartment with another

girl. I'll tell her something. I don't care what she thinks. She'll leave me alone."

"Ray won't like it either."

"He'll find another girl. One who'll fit in the split-level a little better. He'll live."

Joe Milani had no comment.

"I'm just a virgin," she said slowly. "I won't know what to do. But if we go to your place now you can show me, and tomorrow I can move in after I tell my grandmother something. And—"

"Are you very sure, Anita?"

She started to say yes and then she changed her mind. Because she was not at all certain and she saw no reason to conceal her uncertainty from him. "Of course not," she said. "I'm not certain about anything. I'm all mixed up inside and I'm going to pop any minute. Now stop asking me questions. I know what I want right now. I want you to take me home and make love to me. That's all I want."

He stood up, held out a hand for her. She hesitated only for a second. Then she took his hand and straightened up and they began walking out of the park.

When Joe and Anita slipped into the small apartment together, he could not help but sense a vague uneasiness.

Shank was there, sitting on his bed, a paperback novel in one hand. His eyes flicked from the book to the girl, then to Joe, and back to the girl. His lips never moved. His eyes somehow signified he recognized and remembered the girl, and was reserving judgment.

"Shank," Joe said. "Anita."

That was the introduction. Anita smiled at Shank, hesitantly, and Shank nodded shortly before returning to the book. Joe was disturbed by the feeling he could swing either with Shank or Anita—but the three of them?

"Shank—"

Eyes came up. Hard, cold.

"Could you do a brief split?" Joe said.

"Huh?"

"If I give you a quarter will you go to the movies? A little brother routine. Like that."

"Oh," Shank said. "Really?" He stood up, smiled strangely, and closed the novel, tucking it away in his hip pocket. He took out a cigarette and lit it, dropping the match to the floor. "Congratulations," he said, speaking the words to Joe while his eyes were busy reassessing Anita. He had bold eyes. He stared hard at her breasts and loins until she flushed. Then he smiled, pleased, and headed for the door. He left it open and Joe had to close it.

Then he walked over and put his arm around Anita. "I'm sorry," he said.

She raised her head.

"Messy," he said. "Shank can be relatively evil. A mean stud."

"I don't like him," Anita said quietly.

"I do."

"Because he supports you?"

Joe grinned. "Hey," he said. "Like let's not go moralistic, huh? I like Shank. We swing together. I don't want to throw stones at him, Anita. I'm not entirely without sin, you know, and I don't want to cast the first one. Or the second. We get along. We share a pad, talk, hit the same sets."

"I'm sorry."

He led her over to the bed and they sat down together. He tried to figure out what he should do next. The pad was a mess—dirty clothes on the floor, a layer of dirt covering everything. Not romantic, but he didn't suppose that made much difference. It was not the setting itself but the prevailing mood that unnerved him. He and the girl were together in a room she had never been in before to do something she had never done before.

Shank had left, sneering, aware of the agenda. Now Joe was scheduled to make some sort of pass at her, at which she ought to respond avidly. Thereupon they were supposed to make mad and passionate love among the dirt and debris of the apartment.

Then he would go to sleep, or turn on, or go for a walk, or see some people, or do something. And she would board the train for Harlem and say hello to grandma and fall asleep in her own little bed.

It wasn't going to work, Joe thought.

"Look," he said, feeling terribly awkward. "Look, you can call this off. We can stop here and say good-bye. Or we can sit around and talk."

She started. "Did I do something wrong?"

"No," he said. "But—"

"If I did it was an accident. I…I want you to make love to me. That's all."

"We could wait until tomorrow. You could relax a little and then—"

"Tonight."

He digested that. He still did not know where to begin, but he decided that there had to be a way, that all girls were built the same, that somehow they would wind up making their own kind of love. Then, he felt certain, she would go back to Harlem never to return. Sex was one thing. Commitment to an emptiness far greater than the one she spoke of was another.

So Joe put his arm around Anita again and this time he kissed her, quietly. Her mouth stayed closed, but after a moment of the gentle pressure of one pair of lips upon another, her young arms curled around him and held him very close. He liked the taste of her lips, their coolness, and he imagined the sweetness of her young body.

He kissed her again and her lips opened, his tongue turning up between them. Without trying as yet to arouse her, he wanted to know her, to understand her body with his, to touch her in some way not strictly sexual. He kissed her again and he felt the vague fore-shadowings of response—the indrawn breath, the muscular tension and faint quiverings.

"Scared?" Joe said.

Startled, she looked up at him, as if he had been reading her mind.

"This is your ball game," he assured her. "You can call the shots. So there's nothing to be scared of."

And, because there was nothing in the world to say after that, he kissed the girl. He leaned against her a little and they rolled back on the bed. They were lying on their sides, facing one another. He kissed her closed eyes, and kissed her nose. He pressed his lips to her throat, the softness there surprising him. He kissed her again and again.

Then his hand finger-tipped her breast, pliant through the clothing. She stiffened a little. He remembered that this had been as much as the square cat, the engineer, had accomplished in many months of dating. So he held her breast very gently and kissed her again.

He released her. "The light," he explained, and he crossed the room to kill the lamp. The room was plunged into a kind of charcoal gray. He walked back and stretched out next to the girl curled up on the bed like a sleepy kitten in front of a fire, her eyes still closed.

Joe could dimly feel the outline of the white bra through Anita's white sweater. For a time he stroked and fondled. Then, slowly, he pulled the sweater free from the skirt and slipped his hand beneath to rub her back, the small of her back and her shoulders. He found the bra clasp and mastered it.

"Oh," she said. "Oh—"

He kissed her lips. He used both hands to draw the sweater over her head. He could feel the tension in her body. He knew that nobody, no man, at least, had ever seen her breasts before. He knew that exposure scared her, and that he would have to be gentle.

When he had removed the white sweater, he folded it carefully on a chair. He gazed at her bare and lovely breasts, large and firm, crisscrossed by light blue veins, and the nipples miniature red puffs newly wrinkled.

Joe stroked her cool breasts gently, thoughtfully; he was happily aware of her sensual response, but he was sensitive at the same time to a reluctance in that very response that might be welling out of fear. He felt both desire and restraint increasing in Anita and struggling for supremacy and he wondered which would triumph.

After he had undressed, he kissed her breast again, and then linked a chain of light muzzlings around her. She smiled sleepily and he was glad, feeling you had to keep your sense of humor to enjoy sex; humorless, it could drag you, slow you up.

"Joe…" she whispered. "No more."

"You're very pretty, Anita. Very lovely."

"Do you like my breasts?"

"Very much."

"I like it when you kiss them. It makes me feel… funny. I don't know. Funny and good."

"I like to kiss them."

"Do it some more."

He complied, and as he did so he hurried a hand beneath the folds of her skirt, touching the inevitable roughness of a knee and passing upward to the incredibly fantastic softness of a thigh. She gasped.

Now came the really critical part, for Joe to undress her.

He unhooked and unbelted her skirt and he took it off, his eyes dwelling on the dimly discernible wonder of her beautifully slender legs. He paused for a moment, and then he kissed her belly and thighs.

She again quivered and again Joe felt from the girl the same contradictory pairing of passion and fear.

Now she was nude and utterly defenseless; and, before he could touch her, her fear moved to the foreground and made her body rigid with shame.

Joe understood, and became motionless.

"You can go home now," he said. "If you want to. We don't have to go through with it, not now, not if you're afraid of it. We can make it some other time, there's lots of time, you can go home now and rest and relax and think about it and then you can come back tomorrow or the next day or not at all, whatever way you want it. But we don't have to make it now, not when you're afraid."

Her eyes opened.

She looked at him, at his nakedness and her eyes held neither shame nor fear. Then she stared down at herself, at her own nakedness, and she smiled a soft and personal smile.

"I want to, Joe."

"Are you sure?"

"I want to," Anita said. "Of course I'm scared, any girl would be, it's natural, I can't help it. But I want to make love, I want to—even if I can't get as excited as I'd like to. I want to, I want you to do it to me, please do it, please—"

Joe touched her breasts, then, sleeping things awakening the instant he found them; and his hand trailed to find the softest warmth of her, bringing her to an apex of life.

Like creatures in the oldest of dreams, they moved bodies toward one another, and they flowed together into one, the girl's pain at first so agonizing that Joe himself ached from it, his head spinning, his eyes balls of lead. But gradually pain subsided and silken, throbbing pleasure claimed her so magically that, when Anita opened her eyes momentarily to scan the great power of her lover, she could have sworn the charcoal gray of the room had become quilted with rosy fire.

Roaches scurried across the wooden floor, ignoring two warm bodies locked in sorcery and sweetness but not quite love.

✿

Andy's Castle, a cubbyhole bar on Houston Street, was close enough to the mainstream of the Village to be a meeting-place, and far enough away to escape the stream of tourists and Village habitues. A jukebox behind the bar blared the pop tunes of the day.

If the place had an Andy, he failed to be in evidence. A woman barkeep, a blowsy female whose dyed red hair tumbled over burly shoulders, was drawing a stein of draft beer for a rheumy-eyed man.

A boy in the booth at the back very nearly jumped when Shank pushed in through the heavy brown door. The boy forced himself to be calm while Shank ordered a glass of draft.

"Man," the boy said. "Man."

Shank looked at him.

"I been waiting an hour," the boy said. "An hour in this hole. A fucking hour, you dig?"

"Shut up."

"An hour. And—"

Shank started to stand up. The alarm in the boy's face was so great Shank wanted to laugh. Instead, he leaned over and placed his hands on the table in the booth, peering down at the boy.

"You want to play? You want to talk? Or maybe you want to deal," Shank said.

"All right. Cool. Sit down," the boy said.

Shank sat down. "An hour is an hour," he told him. "I'm the one who holds. I'm the one with the world looking at him hard. You can sit in this hole till you rot and you won't get busted for it. Perfectly legal. You're hardly even drinking."

The boy started to say something, but Shank motioned him to shut up.

"You wait for me," Shank went on, "and everything's fine. Everything stays fine. I ever have to wait for you and it's bad. Very ugly. So you do the waiting and you keep cool about it. You dig?"

The boy nodded.

"How much?" Shank asked.

"Twenty cents," the boy said.

Shank nodded. He took out a manila envelope containing two-thirds of an ounce of marijuana and one-third of an ounce of catnip. The boy was a steady customer and bought an average of an ounce a week. It wouldn't do, Shank thought, to put him on a Bull Durham mix. But cutting it slightly with catnip hurt nobody, Shank judged, confident that neither the boy nor the boy's customers, whoever they might be, could tell catnip from marijuana.

"The bread," he said.

A hand reached under the table. Shank took four bills from the hand. He glanced at them. Four fives. Twenty cents, in his parlance. Twenty dollars to the square world. He folded the money and pocketed it.

Then he passed the envelope back the same way. The boy took it and found a pocket for it. Shank noticed the automatic and unconscious change in the boy's expression. He was holding now, violating the law, and a mask of wariness jelled on his face. The boy was the hunted one now.

He made as if to rise.

"Sit down," Shank said. "You waited an hour. Another minute won't hurt."

The boy looked uncomfortable.

"It's good stuff," Shank assured him. "The Mau-Mau's final batch. You don't have to worry."

"Solid."

"About selling it, I mean. Your customers will dig it. You never get beat stuff from the Mau-Mau."

The boy flushed. "I don't sell, Shank."

"Sure, I'm hip. You smoke an ounce a week all by yourself. Solid."

"Shank—"

"You want to lie, it's your business. But don't expect me to believe you."

The boy had a red face now. "Just to come out even," he said. "So my own stuff doesn't cost me anything. That's all."

"I'm hip."

"I don't make a profit. I'm not a…pusher, for Christ's sake."

Shank smiled, happy. "Nobody's a pusher," he said. "We're all connections. Just a big string of connections from the top to the bottom. You're part of a system, my man. That's all. How does it feel to be a little cog in the world's roundest wheel?"

Shank walked out first, letting the kid worry about it. He felt good getting outside. It was the second sale of the night and also the last. He was not holding and he was not hustling anything. Just relaxing. Just walking around and having his own private laughs.

Like the chick. Anita. That was a laugh, a big round one. The two of them balling now, with the chick scared out of her bra and Joe looking like Papa Professor with phallic overtones. Oh, that was a gas.

But the chick was nice. Fine stuff. Choice. He liked the type—the face, the whole flip structure. And he liked the fear. The scared ones were the most fun.

Pretty soon, he thought, he would have to try his luck with her. And he laughed a loud laugh echoing in an alleyway and bouncing back and forth between the empty storefronts of Houston Street. Because it would be very funny. Very funny.

She was on the train heading for home, by herself, naturally. But she had been somewhat astonished that Joe had walked her to the subway. Someone like Ray, naturally, would have escorted her home as a matter of course. But Joe was not Ray, and as a result she had been a little amazed that he had taken the time and trouble to walk her to the Lexington IRT stop at Astor Place.

Now the train rolled north, grinding down the tracks toward Harlem, and she had only her thoughts and memories. It was close to midnight, late for a night before a school day, but she felt no anxiety. Her grandmother would be asleep and probably without worry. Her grandmother seemed to be losing a little more contact with reality every day.

Tomorrow, when Anita would inform the old woman she would be moving out, the girl would scarcely encounter an argument.

Leaving Harlem. Moving in on Saint Marks Place. And where, little girl, are we headed? Where will we wind up, and why?

You are no longer a virgin, little girl, and that, if nothing else, would shock the daylights out of your grandmother. It has even shocked you a bit, little girl, much as you would like to hide the fact. Shocked you to the very core.

Anita smiled that same private and personal smile she had smiled once before that evening. And she remembered the magic of making love, of taking pleasure, giving pleasure and straining for happiness. She had not quite reached the peak, but she had found pleasure enough without it.

And Joe had assured her that she would eventually reach the peak. Not that that as yet made much difference to her; the physical pleasure remaining secondary. Her joy at the total experience was the important matter.

Now she and Joe would live together. So many things would go to hell, she mused—school and home and Ray and that split-level in suburbia. But so much would be left. A new world. Maybe the right one. Because somewhere there had to be the right one, the best of all the possible ones. Somewhere.

After the love-making Joe had offered her a marijuana cigarette that she had declined. And he had shrugged, to show it had not mattered, and had put the cigarette away. She wondered which parts of the life she would take and which to reject. There must be that level to attain on which you could freely search and think without dissipating yourself into the void. She would find that balance and so would Joe.

The train rushed on, from stop to stop, and she rushed along with it. Her thoughts and memories caught her up and whirled her around and she forgot the train and her destination. She all but missed her stop. But as the train pulled into 116th Street, she remembered who she was and where she was and where she was going.

She stepped out of the train and walked up to the night and headed quickly home.

6

A Sunday, and a bad one…rain lashing against the windows…no sun…the air warm in spite of the rain…muggy.

The three people at the makeshift table in the small apartment on Saint Marks Place made a unique family group. They were finishing breakfast. A cigarette burned to ashes between Anita Carbone's fingers. Another dropped from the corner of Joe Milani's mouth. And Shank swallowed the last of his coffee.

The three had been living together in a strange act of communal living for little more than a week. Anita shared Joe's bed. For several days the presence of another man in the room had been disconcerting to Anita. It had been incredibly difficult for her to relax in love when another heart had been beating across the room, another ear possibly listening to the rhythm of love-making. But she had at last grown accustomed to Shank's presence; and when he slept she and Joe made love.

Shank put down his coffee. "Got to move," he said. "Got to see a man."

Joe looked up. "Who?"

Shank shrugged. "A man. Short or tall, fat or thin. I don't know who he is or what he looks like. All I got is a name—Basil. You know, I don't believe there's any-body named Basil. It's impossible."

"A connection?"

"Call it a possibility. Call it a notion. I don't know. They busted Mau-Mau and they put the lid on as tight as it gets around here. It gets hot and it gets cool. Cycles. Junk has as many cycles as sunspots. It gets hot and it gets cool and I wish to hell it would come on a little cooler."

Joe put out his cigarette. "Basil," he said.

"Basil. A name with no face. I don't know. He hangs out in the Kitchen. Hell's Kitchen. Midtown West Side. I go over there and I connect with him, I guess. No-body knows who he is. He buys and sells. That's all I know."

"When do you find him?"

"Today," Shank said. "Today, unless the bastard closes on Sundays. He shouldn't. Business as usual seven days a week in the junk business. He hangs in a coffee pot on West Thirty-ninth. Maybe."

"There's always tomorrow."

Shank shook his head. "I ran into Judy," he said. "I got a set to supply tomorrow night. So I have to meet Basil today. Life is filled with responsibilities." He smiled, more to himself than to Joe and Anita. He was beginning to enjoy coming on with philosophical phrases. You sounded deep and people put you up for it, Shank thought.

"A set?" Anita asked.

"A party," Joe answered Anita. "At Judy Obershain's. She's a good little chick. Sick, but a good chick. Her parties move nicely."

"Are we going," Anita wanted to know.

"Might as well," Joe said. "Be some good people there. Be best if Shank scores with this Basil cat. Judy's parties can be a bring-down if there's nothing to ease the pain."

Shank stood up slowly. He wandered around the room, found a leather jacket and put it on. "Rain," he said. "God, I hate rain. One thing about the coast, you didn't get rain like this. If it rained it did it and got done. None of this slow rain that stays around all day."

"Wait for it to clear a little," Joe suggested.

"Hell with it. Basil won't wait. The world won't wait. Life is a collection of unbearable demands. Later for all of you."

And Shank was gone. Anita crossed the room to close the door and then returned to Joe.

"I hope he scores," Joe said.

"I hope he doesn't," Anita blurted.

Joe gave her an odd look. "Really? What's bugging you?"

"I don't like…pot."

He laughed softly. "How do you know? You never made it, baby."

"I just don't like it."

Joe's voice was lazy. "I can remember when you didn't like sex, baby. Then you turned on to it and you found out it was something fine. You haven't been the same since, you know. Sexiest woman around."

Anita started to grin, but then shook her head. "I still don't like pot," she said. "I don't have to try it to know I don't like it."

"What don't you like about it?"

"What it does to you. It takes you far away from me. It makes you so…I don't know. Cool. Distant. As though you're miles and miles away. As though there's a thick glass wall around you, so that you can see out and I can see in but I can't touch you. And a really thick wall, so that the images are a little warped."

"You talk fine. Poetic, sort of."

"Joe—"

"You can tear down the wall, baby. You can turn yourself on and come inside where it's warm and cozy."

"Joe—"

"I'm a permissive cat," he went on. "Very easy to get along with. You want to stay straight, that's your business. I don't try to turn you on. I don't try to run your life. You go where you want and you do what you want. It's up to you. You want to smoke a stick or two, that's all right with me—we can smoke together and swing together and take a quiet trip way to the top. You don't want to, fine. Solid. So you be permissive. So don't try to run my life. It's my life, baby."

"I know it, Joe."

"Then show it. You know how many times you told

me you don't like pot? It can get on a cat's nerves. Really, baby. You can become a drag."

"I'm sorry."

"Like yesterday. Like walking out of the pad because I was turning on and you didn't want to be around. That wasn't nice. Anti-social."

"I—"

"A lot of cats would have insisted you make the scene yourself. I'm not like that. Hell, it's not like we're married, for God's sake. We just swing together. All right. So you don't have to smoke and I don't have to stop."

"I'm sorry," she said. "I'm…sorry."

He relaxed. "I'm going out for a walk," Joe said. "Just a little walk."

"In the rain?"

"I won't melt. The pad has me all confined today. Like a prison. I'll be back in a while."

"Can I come?"

He hesitated. "You stay here," he said. "I got thinking to do. I can do it better alone."

Her disappointment showed in her face. "Oh," she said. "Will you be gone long?"

"God," he said. "I told you, a little while. Just stay here and maybe straighten up a little and I'll be back. God, I told you—"

"I'm sorry," she said again.

Joe gave the girl a quick kiss on the forehead, forced a smile and quit the apartment. When he hit the street he at once felt better—liberated, as if he had escaped.

The rain did not trouble him; it slanted down lightly now, a fine spray. Joe strode through without difficulty. He hurried to Second Avenue, then walked to a small East Side coffee house called Bird In Hand. It was dark inside. The front part contained half a dozen tables, and a back room had four more. It was to the back that Joe walked, where he took a table close to the adjoining kitchen. For a moment he was completely alone, until the waitress approached for his order.

The waitress, a thin, hollow-eyed blonde named Eileen, wore tight dungarees and a loose-fitting black sweater. Joe grinned, reaching to pat her buttocks. He had slept with her once or twice several months ago and had liked her.

"Coffee," he said. "American coffee, black, no sugar. And if somebody's looking for a chess game, here I am. Ready and willing."

"Solid," Eileen said. "You've been absent lately."

"Miss me?"

"Like I miss a boil. Busy?"

"Not too." Joe shrugged.

"There's a set at Judy's. Going?" Eileen asked.

"I think so. Tomorrow night?"

"That's the one."

She headed for the kitchen and returned with a cup of coffee. Joe handed her a quarter and she pocketed it in her dungarees; then she sighed heavily and sat down opposite him. "God, I'm dragged," she said. "This is a bitch of a day."

"What's wrong?"

"Everything. You know Dave?"

"Dave Schwerner?"

"That's the one. I've been living with him."

"I'm hip."

"Well, he's been playing needle games," she complained.

Joe shook his head. "Bad," he said. "Horse?"

"Uh-huh. Just skin-popping. That's all, he says. Just skin-popping. He can take it or leave it. Funny, you know. Because he can take it or leave it but he never leaves it. Isn't that funny?"

Joe said nothing.

"So we're always broke," she went on. "But very broke. I don't make much here, you know that. A buck an hour plus a tip now and then. And he spends long bread on the needle. Nobody goes through money like a junkie."

"Hold on," Joe said. "He's not a junkie."

"Then Dave's faking it. So he's not hooked. He's still using a little too regularly to make me happy. And we're always broke. And you know what comes next."

"He wants you to try a needleful?"

"Not that. Not yet. I suppose that's next on the agenda but he can go to hell for himself before I punch needle-holes in myself. No, another brainstorm. We're sitting around, wondering how to pay for the next cap of heroin, and he mentions a way we could be rolling in bread."

"Oh."

"You got it," she said. "The same old story. *I was thinking, honey*, Dave says. *You know, all you would have to do is turn one little trick a day and we'd be living in style. An extra fifteen bucks a day. Pay for the horse and money left over to live on. Not that you would be professional or anything. I wouldn't want that. Just one little trick a day.*"

Joe kept silent.

"And then he's using more horse," Eileen went on, "and then it's two little tricks a day, and then all of a sudden he's mainlining with thirty or forty pounds worth of monkey, and then I'm on it myself because otherwise it's too much to stand by myself, and there we are, a pair of junkies, and I'm spreading my legs for the world to keep us both alive. *Just one little trick a day*, Dave says. Sure."

"That's bad, Eileen. That's like ugly."

"It gets uglier. Because I don't know what to do, baby. I really don't. I ought to leave him. Somebody hits the needle and you have to forget he's alive. But he needs me, Joe. And I don't know what to do. He needs me. It's a funny feeling, when somebody needs you. And one of these days I'm going to turn that one little trick. And I don't want to. I really don't want to."

Joe started to say something but then suddenly knew comment to be hopeless.

Eileen heaved a sigh and stood up. "Problems," she said. "Everybody's got them. If we didn't have them we wouldn't be here. Stay good, Joe. I'm going to pour coffee for the savages. Later."

He watched her go. He thought about Eileen turning tricks to feed Dave's habit and he felt very sad. It was ugly. But so were lots of things. The world was growing very ugly. Problems? He had problems of his own.

Funny problems.

Anita problems.

You had a woman now, Joe brooded. And when you had a woman you had problems. Things were most assuredly not the same. There were strings all over the place. There were things you couldn't do.

You couldn't hit on another chick. You couldn't stay out all night. You couldn't get quite as stoned as you used to and you couldn't live quite as completely within yourself.

Not that you necessarily wanted to hit on another chick, to find another bed to warm. Anita was fine in that department, alive and exciting, enough for any man. But the simple fact that you couldn't if you wanted to, was enough to annoy the hell out of you.

The big headache was that Anita just didn't fit in. It was not her scene, not at all. She was too sane for it, maybe. Not sick enough to throw herself headlong into the hysteria of hipdom. Maybe she should have stayed in Harlem and married her split-level engineer. Because a cold-water hole on Saint Marks Place was not her speed.

What was her speed? Joe frowned.

And where was the whole bit headed? Where in the world were Anita and you going, and what in the world would you do when you got there?

Joe sipped his coffee. After a while Lee Revzin came in carrying a chess set. The poet sat down without a word. He took a white pawn in one hand, a black pawn in the other. He mixed them up, then extended both closed fists to Joe. Joe tapped one and got white. They set up the pieces and began to play.

They played for three hours. In the course of the several games Lee said only two words, *"Check,"* when Joe's king was in check, and *"Mate,"* when he won a game. When Lee had something to say he could talk non-stop for hours. One time he had exploded in spontaneous poetry for an hour and a half, talking in perfect heroic couplets and hitting some astonishingly successful and vivid images. At other times he would go for days without uttering a syllable.

Joe matched the poet's silence with his own. He played chess and drank coffee and let his mind live a life by itself.

Basil was hard to find.

A check of available coffee pots in the area yielded nothing. Shank was having a hard time. He was also beginning to feel thoroughly annoyed.

The Kitchen was a fairly dismal slum but this failed

to dismay Shank. Nor did the slum's inhabitants—
Irish, Italian, and a sprinkling of Puerto Ricans—
affect Shank either. But the juveniles of the area were
another story. He was close enough to them in age to
be a possible member of an alien gang. At one point
two teeners approached him, their eyes wary. He was
on their turf, and that might to them mean an invasion. Shank remembered the protocol of the Royal
Ramblers and now the routine struck him as ridicu-
lous. But Shank knew the language and he was ready.

"Who are you, man?"

He looked the taller of the two in the eyes. "I'm
looking for Basil," he said. "You know him?"

Shank read the expression. They knew Basil. But
they were too small to deal with him. Basil was big and
they were little. They bought what they used, if they
used, from someone not nearly so tall as Basil. Someone like Shank, perhaps.

"You got business with him?" the taller one said.

"I buy," Shank said. "I sell."

"You swing with a gang?"

"Years ago but no more."

It was satisfactory. They let him alone because they
knew he was not in their way. But they did not know
Basil's whereabouts.

Nobody did. The mystery was becoming a drag.
Finally Shank entered the coffee pot where, by all the
rules, Basil should have been. Shank sauntered to the

counter and studied the girl behind it. He asked for Basil and her eyes informed him she knew both the name and the man.

"I don't know him," the girl said.

"Call him." Shank said. "Tell him somebody wants to see him."

"I don't know him."

"Crap," Shank said. "You pour me a cup of coffee. Cream and sugar. Then you get your butt over to the phone and you call him. Fast."

"I don't know you," she said. "Maybe you're law."

"I look like law?"

She shrugged.

But for the girl and Shank, the diner was empty. Shank walked around the counter and moved in on the girl. She seemed vaguely frightened but obviously did not know what to do next. There was nobody to call on for help.

Shank took out the knife. He sprang the blade, and the girl's eyes widened. He moved the blade until it was about an inch away from her stomach.

"Law doesn't carry blades," he said. "But you go right on thinking I'm law, and you go right on giving me a hard time. Then I'll have to prove to you I'm not law. You know how I'll do it?"

Her mouth made an O.

"I'll cut your glands," he said succinctly. "Wouldn't you rather call Basil?"

She nodded. She started for the phone.

"First the coffee. Cream and sugar."

She poured the coffee. Then she found the phone and dropped a dime into it and dialed. He sat at the counter and sipped coffee, pleased.

"He's on his way," she told him.

Shank nodded. He waited. Less than five minutes later the man called Basil stepped into the diner. He was a small man, five-and-a-half feet short, small-boned, bald. He had nervous eyes. He was well-dressed and over-dressed, as many small men are. His hat was black and short-brimmed, his topcoat an expensive tweed. His Italian loafers were highly shined.

"You wanted to see me?" Basil's voice was low.

Shank nodded. "Can we go somewhere?"

"First let me know who you are."

"You can call me Shank."

"I never made that handle."

"You do now. You used to know somebody named Mau-Mau. So did I."

"Ancient history," Basil said.

"That's the point. You also know a guy named Billy-Billy and a girl named Joyce. So do I."

"Billy-Billy's a fine fellow," Basil said thoughtfully. "He and Joyce make a good couple."

"Billy-Billy's gay as a jay," Shank said. "Joyce is a hustler for somebody uptown. Do I pass?"

"You pass," Basil said, amused. "Follow me."

They walked along 39th Street to Tenth Avenue, turned up Tenth to 40th, then down 40th to a crumbling brownstone. A sign announced the building had been condemned. Large white Xs adorned the windows.

They entered the building and climbed three flights. Basil put a key into a lock, turned it. They walked into an empty room where, obviously, no one lived. But here Basil kept his goods. The place was known as a drop— a place for the storage, exchange, sale and delivery of junk.

"What do you want?" Basil asked.

"Pot."

Basil shrugged. "I hardly carry it," he said. "No profit. I'm surprised you bother. You swing with Billy-Billy and Joyce, you ought to have something better going for you. Pot is small-time. Very small. Not tall at all."

"I get along."

"You could get along better."

"And sell hard stuff?"

Basil nodded.

"I don't like hard stuff," Shank said. "They bust you for hard stuff and they lay it on you. Hard. Jails sort of drag me. I don't like them."

"You go to the same jails for pot," Basil said. "The law doesn't know the difference. Look at the Mau-Mau. Three times was the charm for him. And he never sold a grain of powder."

"Maybe."

"You could handle both," Basil said. "Pot for the teaheads, horse for the live ones. More money in it."

"I've got a steady clientele."

"With heroin, customers look for you. A captive audience. No hustling, no worry. If you just want pot you can look for another connection. To tell you the truth, I just carry it as a service. I wouldn't sell it alone. But I'll sell it along with the other. And I can make a nice price."

Shank thought about it. There was one big point in Basil's favor. The law saw no difference between marijuana and heroin. The law was stupid. And you might as well hang for a sheep as a lamb.

"How nice a price?"

"You sell for five cents a cap. I let you have it for two. A profit of three. Tax-free, baby."

A nice price, Shank judged, and he said, "I've got fifty dollars. Name me a list of goods."

"Fifty?" Basil considered. "Twenty caps," he said. "And two ounces of gauge. I lose money on the gauge that way. But you're new. It's a favor."

Two ounces was not enough, Shank thought quickly. Not with the party the next night.

"Fifteen caps and three ounces," he said.

Basil frowned. "Baby," he said. "Baby, how much money do you want me to lose?"

"I need three ounces."

They talked about it. And finally Basil agreed. "But

you'll learn," he said. "You'll drop the pot after a while. One of your customers gets picked up and he'll tip them to you without thinking. He won't be a junkie. He won't need to protect you. And there you are, lover. Busted because you sell pot. That doesn't happen when you sell junk. They don't do a pigeon routine. They don't dare. They don't want to be cut off cold. They don't want to risk a hot shot. You know from a hot shot?"

Shank knew. But Basil explained anyway.

"I saw it happen," he said. "A long-tailed rat. Turned in his pusher to cop a plea. He tried to connect with somebody else, somebody who knew the score. He got his. He got a cap of strychnine. Heated it on his spoon and sent it home and died with the needle in his arm. Ugly, baby."

They ironed out the deal. Basil gave Shank three envelopes, each having an ounce of marijuana. Then he handed Shank another envelope containing fifteen capsules of heroin. Shank counted out ten five-dollar bills.

"A pleasure," the little man said. He put away the money and smiled. "You know where I hang. The afternoon's the best time. Find me at leisure. Keep my name a secret. Don't talk in your sleep. And don't become your own customer. I won't sell to you once you become a user yourself. Smoke all the pot you want. Start riding the horse and I cut you off clean.

I don't sell to junkies. I've got a code of ethics. No morals. But loads of ethics."

Shank left first. He walked away from the condemned brownstone and headed east. He walked two blocks, then jumped in a cab and gave the driver his address.

He kept peering out the back window. There was no tail and he was very glad. He felt hotter than a stove and the heroin was burning a hole-and-a-half in his pocket. He did not feel at all safe until the heroin and the pot were stashed away in the apartment. Both Anita and Joe were elsewhere when he arrived, which relieved Shank because he sensed it a good idea they remain unaware of the presence of heroin.

7

Party time.

Judy Obershain had money. Her father, a well-to-do Boston businessman, sent her a healthy check once a month to keep Judy out of Boston. He loved his daughter—reservedly, but sincerely—and he knew well enough it would be better all across the board if he and Judy saw each other as little as possible. So the small, gaminish girl used her monthly manna to inhabit an apartment in the West Village and to experience all the kicks available, with the exception, oddly, of the act of losing her virginity. Long ago, when Judy's mother had been among the living, that good woman had explained again and again to Judy how terrible it would be to cease being a virgin. Judy's mother, a frigid witch if there ever had been one, had succeeded admirably. Judy, as promiscuous and perverted a girl as one could hope to find anywhere, had remaind a virgin.

Now Judy's four-room apartment was being devoted to a party. The party was moving nicely. Several gallons of sour red wine were being passed from person to person, and the twenty or so people present were busy getting as high as they could. Judy was happy. The marijuana, purchased from Shank at a cost of a hundred dollars, would soon be brought out and consumed.

And from there on the party would become a real blast. Nothing could have pleased Judy more. She liked a party that moved.

She was sitting on the couch now. Next to her a boy and girl were busy with a gallon of wine; periodically, the boy's hand would fondle her breast. Judy was pleased. The sexier a party became, the better it was.

Judy closed her eyes, remembering one magnificent party where everybody had gone shriekingly high on mescalin. That particular blast had been an orgy that would have delighted Nero. It had certainly delighted Judy. At one superb point she and another girl had delighted a particular boy—and the effect had been exhilarating.

Thinking about that began to warm Judy. Here we go again, she thought. Life is just a bowl of cherries. And I am one of them.

A boy passed. He had a full beard, long hair, rather wild eyes. His name was Nick Long and his prowess was legendary, and Judy was intent either on proving or disproving it.

She caught at his arm. "Sit down," she said. "I'm lonesome."

Nick looked at her, considered, sat down.

"You and I," she said, "really ought to get acquainted. You've got to pay attention to the hostess. It's the first rule of genteel party-going."

"If we were in a room all by ourselves," he said, "then I could really pay attention to you."

"Yeah?"

"Uh-huh. You look nice, baby. I could ball with you and enjoy it. We could both enjoy it."

"You're hot stuff, huh?"

"The best."

She grinned like a monkey. "There are ground rules," she said. "Rules of the house."

"I've heard."

"The word is rather widespread," she admitted. "The rules suit you?"

"They might," he said. "I hear you're a woman of the world."

"Then let's go."

They got up and she tucked her arm in his. Nobody paid any particular attention to them as they left the party and found a bedroom temporarily unoccupied.

When Judy and Nick returned to the party the wine had all but been consumed, which meant only it was time to break out the pot. Judy had already rolled it that afternoon and she brought out the cigarettes with glee the party-goers shared unanimously with the exception of Anita Carbone. Pot continued to repel Anita; she disliked the party, too, for that matter. She wanted to go home.

But Anita said nothing about her wish. She knew Joe wouldn't like it at all. As a matter of fact, Joe had lately become increasingly critical of her. Nothing she did seemed to please him. She could not be sure of what might be wrong. Sometimes he apparently thought she was too square, while at other times he told her she was trying too hard to be hip, and still other times…

But it was hard to say, really, exactly what was bothering Joe. He would tell her she was trying to run his life. Well, she mused, maybe she was trying to impose her will on him. She didn't want to, certainly, but it was hard for her to weigh whether she was or no.

She had discovered one thing. Her escape had been one from something rather than to something else. She had run away from the twin beacons of Harlem and Long Island, but she had not reached anything satisfyingly conclusive. The life she and Joe had become involved in had not yielded anything particularly characteristic. Actually, a lack of values predominated.

Perhaps this very lack of values, Anita reflected, might be enough—for the time being, at least—and give her a chance to breathe, while she could discover what she really wanted, what niche in life she could comfortably occupy. For the first time, Anita felt she should think of her life with Joe as a temporary thing, and not as an end in itself.

She let her gaze rove about the room. Judy was passing out the cigarettes—no sooner offered than eagerly snatched. These people, Anita thought. The ones who said: *This is the life, this is what it's all about.* They were wrong, she felt. They had to be wrong. They made such a great show of not caring what other people thought, and yet they were so desperately concerned with coming on strong. In rejecting the values of a society they couldn't cope with, they had made the drastic mistake of setting up their own society—every bit as illogical as the one they had rebelled against. And they had bowed to their own society's false values while they had rejected a little too vehemently the false values of the repudiated society.

And there Anita stood, dead center. And not knowing which way to turn, because no path seemed open.

Where next?

"Anita—" Joe began.

She turned.

"You going to smoke, baby?" he said, his tones gentle.

His face played with a smile. Her failure to open the doors to the sky via marijuana amused him more than it annoyed him. His half-teasing, half-coaxing commentary continued.

"You don't have to, baby. But you better not breathe too deep. All these people smoking, they'll get you high by being in the same room. Just a little high, but high. And with the wine you've been drinking you just might get an edge on. A little burn, like. You want that to happen? What do you say, baby?"

Lee Revzin, the poet, was lighting up a joint in the corner. He held the flame to the twisted end of the cigarette and drew in deeply. Then he passed the joint to a girl with long red hair whose name Anita did not know.

"Or do you want to go home?" Joe asked. "You could pick up your marbles and go home, baby. Play it safe. Go all the way home, to grandma. You might dig that. You could tell that Ray Rico cat what a wild life you've been leading. Impress the hell out of him."

He was being very nasty now and the words hurt her. But still she knew that he did not really mean them. He had wanted to make love before the party and she hadn't felt like it. So he was taking out his frustrations on her, whipping her with his unsatisfied maleness. She did not like it but she could not blame him for it.

"I'll smoke," she said.

"Really?"

"Really." But why? She asked herself. She didn't want to. Or did she? And if so, why? Maybe to share more of his world. Maybe to sink herself further. Maybe because she needed him more than she wanted to admit. Maybe because, for some irrational reason, she was beginning to feel something for him she didn't want to name. Maybe love.

Joe held a joint between his thumb and forefinger and smiled at Anita. "Hemp," he said. "Tea, gauge, grass. A million names for a million games. Let's blow up, little girl."

He lit it and took the first drag, then handed it to

her. She needed no instructions. She had seen him do it and she had watched Shank.

So she took the cylinder of marijuana and put it in her mouth. She drew the mixture of smoke and air deep, deep, deep into her lungs. It did not taste pleasant and she wanted to cough. But it was a sin to cough, to waste the smoke forever, so she held on to it. It stayed down until she had to let out her breath, by which time he had passed the joint back to her for another drag.

The high came gradually, reaching Anita before she became aware of it. Living with Joe in an environment of which marijuana had been part of the day-by-day routine, she had grown to believe that pot itself was largely a state of mind, that the weed affected you only if you worked the effect up all by yourself. A sort of auto-hypnosis, the way she had understood it. As a result, the effect marijuana now had upon her was rather startling.

She closed her eyes and thought, nevertheless, that she could see. An illusion, of course, and she recognized it as such, but it was nonetheless enjoyable.

Her body felt dynamically alive, every muscle a substance she could see, hear, feel. She listened to the blood rushing through veins and arteries, and quivered to the softness of her enveloping clothing. A record, loaded with flamenco music, played full blast, and she not only heard each note but the space between them as well.

She felt Joe's hand on her arm and her whole body wakened to his touch. Suddenly she wanted him, wanted him more than ever, sex more beckoning than it had ever been before. She itched and throbbed with desire.

"Joe…" She muttered.

His arms circled her from behind, his hands kneading her breasts. It occurred to her that everybody could witness her and Joe, but it also occurred to her that she did not care. The sensations were delicious, far more so than they ever had been. Her eyes were clenched tightly shut, and every square inch of her tingled with the joy caused by his wonderful, marvelous hands.

"My sweater, Joe," she said. "Take it off. Touch me, touch me, it feels so good, so fine, so wonderfully fine, and I'm high, I'm way up in the air, way way way up in the air—"

Joe took off her sweater, the air cool on her bare breasts.

The air.

Then his hands.

She even imagined she could sense the pattern of his fingerprints as he fondled her warm breasts in his warm hands.

It felt divine.

After several eternities he released her. And, her eyes still clenched tightly shut, she felt him spin her lazily around to her back.

Then, as he crouched over her, her mind reeled. This is vulgar, she thought. This is common, not lady-like at all. What would Grandma think? She would disapprove.

But her sensations were so overwhelmingly exhila-rating...

Anita knew what was happening. Joe was removing her slacks. Not ladylike at all, but so nice...

And then Joe was really making her, through and through, and it wasn't right because there they were in a roomful of people and everybody could see them, movement by movement.

But it felt so good, so velvetly good, and her hips were humming like a dynamo and trying to behave like a centrifuge, whirling, swirling with her good man who felt so good, good, good!

And it got better and better and better until the sky fell in and the world blew up in a shower of stars—you hear me? Stars, stars all over so your body could smile all over at the sight of all your secrets flowing out...

"Let us consider the semantics of Hip," Lee Revzin said. "Let us take the words apart and see the interior of the star-spangled world. Let us probe the quin-tessence of hipness and reduce a subculture to words."

He was seated in an armchair. His eyes were closed, his head angled back. He spoke in a loud, clear voice and did not pause for breath.

"The Hip does not make love," he went on. "The

Hip makes *it*. To make love implies a dualism of motive, a double effort involving two people. So the Hip does not make love. He makes *it*. *It* is individual. It is coeducational jazz with an organic goal in mind. *It* is Reichian, Wilhelm Reichian. Let's all have an orgasm, boys and girls. Let's make it."

The girl put a cigarette in his mouth, struck a match for him. Without opening his eyes he accepted the cigarette and took the light. He inhaled, then blew out the smoke without removing the cigarette from his mouth. He left it there while he spoke.

"Consider the verb *make*. It will reveal unto us, boys and girls, the constructive illusion in a destructive subculture. Make. The universal verb, the inevitable. I can't make it, baby. Let us make another scene. Let us make *it*. Make, make, make. It means everything, anything. A universal. A perfect universal. The unfortunate fact is that it also means nothing at all. Because, boys and girls, nothing is made, created, constructed, built. Make all day and make all night and make nothing. Lord, we fished all night and caught nothing. Lord, we made it all night and we didn't make a mother-loving thing."

The cigarette burned down to his lips while he went on talking and smoking. The girl took the cigarette from him and put it out. She replaced it with a fresh cigarette.

"Then there is the nomenclature of Hip," Lee Revzin said. "Man first, then Baby. Call everybody *man*

and remember no names. Then call everybody baby.
Strangers and afraid in a world we just can't make.
Where are you, Housman? Where is everybody?"

He coughed and the girl took the cigarette away
from him. He smiled gratefully.

"I will recite a poem," he said. "A poem to the world.
A panegyrical paean for the poor peons. A poem, for
the love of the lord, a poem."

He said:

Never is a naughty word
Summer is a winter crutch
Lovers in a cinder block
Make a scene of nothing much.
Captains of the somewhere fleet
Say their prayers and go their ways
Lovers on a vacant roof
Sing the song of sometimes praise.
When the world is upside down
Inside out and also ran
See the prairie horses rush
Sifting gold in frying pan.
Halt the horses of the mind
Still the voice of autumn snakes
When somebody drops the clutch
That's the time to hit the brakes.

The girl applauded wildly.
"There's more," he said. "Then you may applaud.
Beat your hands together with passion. The ego needs

it. Also the id. We will of course omit the super-ego.
We will always omit the super-ego."

He went on in an Epicene and passionless frog-croak:

Slit the skins of silver eggs
Splash the ground that summer sings
Music mourns dead birds
Breath is sweet in broken things.

The girl applauded still more wildly.

"I wish I knew what in the world it means," Lee
Revzin said, more to himself than to the world. "It has
to mean something. It really has to."

The girl said nothing. She was busy unzipping him,
stimulated beyond imagination by the force of his
poetry.

Shank, meanwhile, was bored.

That was surprising. Judy Obershain's parties had
never bored him in the past. The people had inter-
ested him and the activities had appealed.

Now, however, he was bored.

The boredom, he decided, had a number of causes.
For one thing, the thrill of smoking marijuana by way
of being part of a group function no longer served to
send him into the stratosphere. Pot was a part of his
daily life—he bought it, he sold it, he smoked it. He
found it no more delightful to smoke in public than in
private. And the spectacle of twenty or more idiots
blowing their brains out so thoroughly that they lost
control of themselves was humorous no longer.

Another factor was his discovery that, although he was one of the youngest present at the party, the others seemed incredibly immature to him. He attributed this feeling partly to a change in his status. He was selling hard goods now; in fact he had made his first sale just a few hours ago. Basil could talk his head off about the similarity on the legal plane of marijuana and heroin. But Shank's eyes were not those of the law, and for him a radical difference existed between the two drugs, so that he felt immeasurably superior to the idiots balling all over Judy Obershain's apartment. Pot was fine, you could take it or leave it, Shank thought; smoke it on Madison Avenue or the Upper East Side or the Village. But junk was serious business—and pot was for kiddies.

Now he was a businessman. You didn't sell junk for the hell of it, Shank ruminated. You sold it for a profit, a good profit. Moreover, the stuff had a quick turnover and, as Basil had described it, a captive audience. You could make three, four, five bills a week if you were cool about it. And this potential for enormous profits further contributed to raising him above the level of the rest of the party-goers.

Even the sex was dull. Shank gave a mental shrug. He just plain wasn't in the mood and there was no way to force it. The party was dragging him, the people were dragging him, the whole aura of child-play, love-play, sex-play was dragging him.

So he got up, carrying a good load from the pot he had smoked but carrying it easily, understanding it, able to master it with ease. Unlike Anita, who had just tried it for the first time and now was fornicating like a rabbit in the middle of the living-room floor. Shank walked to the door after stepping over a pair of errant lovers, and left the apartment.

The building elevator was the self-service type. But instead of pushing the button for the ground floor, he pressed for the floor below, the third, and headed for the apartment directly below that of Judy Obershain's.

He rang the bell. Rang it once, waited, then leaned on it.

The people were not home.

He opened the door with a key that fitted a surprising number of doors. He walked in, shut the door and began looking around for something to steal. Then, all at once, he decided there was no point to burglarizing the place. He was making enough money. He didn't need any more.

Instead, he used the phone to call Bradley Galton, his stepfather, long distance. When Brad Galton answered, Shank waited for a second or two and then unleashed a stream of the wildest profanity he could think of. He did not pause for breath until the line went dead.

Then, smiling, Shank replaced the receiver and quit the apartment. He hoped the phone call to the coast would come as a great surprise to the people who would be billed for it.

He caught the elevator again, rode it to the first

floor, ambled out into the night and hunted for a bar where he ordered a glass of draft beer and drank it down. He walked all the way home, looking around for anybody he might know. He saw a few people but nobody he wanted to talk to. So he wound up going straight back to the apartment on Saint Marks Place.

But he felt too alert to sleep. He checked the cache of heroin, of which fourteen capsules remained. He checked the marijuana. He had sold Judy Obershain an ounce and had taken one hundred dollars for it, which meant he had two ounces of marijuana left and fourteen caps of horse and was already ahead by more than fifty dollars. A profitable day, he congratulated himself.

His mind returned to Anita.

Something was going to happen, Shank decided. There was more than enough for Joe there. The girl was appealing, and scared, and Shank was going to help himself to a little. Just a little. Not right away, but fairly soon. When he was ready he would simply take what he wanted. If she would not want to give it to him that would be just too damn bad. He would take it anyway.

He undressed and stretched out on his bed. In his mind he concocted pleasant fantasies involving Anita. In one, her ankles were tied together, and her hands bound behind her back. She was shrieking in agony.

He went to sleep and dreamed of pain.

8

They sat on a bench in Washington Square.

Looking at her through the smoke from his cigarette, Joe was amazed at the change time had worked in the girl beside him. Before, Anita had worn a little lipstick; now she dispensed with it altogether and made up for it by wearing too much eye-shadow. Tight and faded dungarees encased belly and hips and legs. A loose black sweater covered her arms and chest. Her hair fell free, loose.

But the outer trappings were the least of the change. Any girl could replace lipstick with eye-shadow, could switch from skirt and sweater to dungarees and sweater, could unpin her hair and let her mouth go slack and her eyes droopy. Such could be accomplished overnight, and frequently was—generally by freshman girls from Brooklyn College making the perfunctory pilgrimage to Greenwich Village before they went home to marry dentists. *Exchange students from Kew Gardens,* Lee Revzin called them. *Kiddie-beats.*

Anita was different. More important than the outer wrapper was the girl inside. And there had been a change in that girl of direction, of attitude and mind. The words of Hip colored her speech now and sounded right coming from her mouth. The exchange students from Kew Gardens, when they used those words, made them sound like English from the lips of a Sudanese.

She walked Hip and thought Hip and spoke Hip. Harlem and Long Island had drained away from her and the beat mystique had quickly replaced them. She accompanied Joe when he wanted her company; other times she remained at the apartment or wandered around the Village and the East Side by herself. She smoked marijuana with Joe, and had tried both codeine cough syrup and mescalin, neither of which had made much of an impression upon her. The cough syrup had merely drugged her for a while until she had unceremoniously thrown it up in the toilet bowl. The mescalin had given a weak high which she had found unpleasant and a bit frightening. But marijuana had seemed valuable, somehow, and she continued to smoke it whenever he did.

Joe looked at her now, his eyes all-seeing, and he thought perhaps he had done something radically wrong. The metamorphosis from Square to Hip was, he knew full well, far from complete. He knew she worried, and he knew she was firmly convinced that much of what she was doing was intrinsically wrong. He remembered her as she had been, fresh and eager and searching for something beyond her comprehension. And he was not at all sure that what she had become was an improvement on the original.

He recalled the first time she had smoked—at Judy's Obershain's party. He remembered their love-making on the floor, more or less center-stage, and he remembered how she had been when the effects of the marijuana had worn off. Scared, sick, frightened— and very much ashamed of herself. Then at last the shame had slipped away and the fear had claimed her altogether. And she was still not a girl who could make love in the middle of the floor in the middle of a party without there being something wrong about it for her, without some guilt that had to be buried beneath the rugged exterior of the perennial cool.

Bad, Joe thought.

"I hate this park," she said now.

"Huh?"

"It drags me," she said. "It really does. I sit here and all these people walk by. It used to be a kick. I mean, I didn't know any of the people. They were strangers. And now either I know them or I've seen them so many times it's like they're relatives or like that. I want something to happen. God, I want something to happen."

"Like what?"

"I don't know."

He dropped his cigarette and stepped on it. A small boy stopped and asked Joe if he wanted his shoes shined. Joe pointed to his tennis sneakers and laughed easily. The boy frowned, laughed and left them to bother somebody else.

"We could go to the coast," he said. "North Beach or something. Everybody goes to the coast. It's like the thing to do."

"I don't want to."

"I mean, if you're hung up on New York—"

"Not New York. Not New York, not the park, I don't know. Just hung up in general, I suppose. Just bored and tired. I don't know."

"A change of scene might help."

"I'm a leopard, Joe."

He stared, feeling disoriented. "A leper? I don't get it, baby. I—"

"Not a leper. A leopard. Like an animal. Leopards can't change their spots. Remember?"

"Oh," he said.

"Allee samee under the skin. New York or Chicago or San Francisco or…I don't know. Portugal. Wherever you run it's the same person running. Can't run out of yourself. Doesn't work."

He said nothing.

"I think I'm going back to the pad," she said.

"Want me to come?"

Anita shook her head no. "I just have eyes to walk. I'm going to buy a big cup of Italian ice from the cat on the corner of Thompson, the funny one with the wagon. And I'm going to walk all the way home eating the ice. Then I'll sit around and wait for you."

Joe shrugged.

"A nice long walk," she said. "In the lovable afternoon. I'll make dinner. Paella, I think. A pot of rice and some seafood. It's cheap and it tastes good. Spanish. I made it last week."

He remembered. "Shank may be around," he said.

"I hope not."

"You really put him down, don't you? He's a good cat. He's making nice bread and giving us our share."

"He's making too much bread."

"Huh?"

"I don't like it," she said. "That's a lot of money from peddling pot. I think he's doing something else. Muggings, hold-ups, I don't know."

"He wouldn't do that."

"He'd do anything," she told him. "My God, you don't know him at all. He's a rotten son of a bitch, Joe. He really is. He's a snake."

He remained silent, having no great drive to spring to Shank's defense. "He never did anything to you," he managed after a few moments.

"I know."

"So why the noise? There's lots of studs I can live without. But I don't go screaming on 'em all the time."

She smiled. It was a strange smile. Then she stood up.

"Later," she said. "Fall up around six or so for dinner. It's okay to reheat it, you can keep the pot on the stove for a week. But it's best the first day."

He watched her walk away until she was out of sight and he wondered what was wrong. She was a leopard and she couldn't change her spots. Solid. But why all the fuss?

He thought about Shank. Somehow he couldn't see Shank as a stick-up man. The picture did not add up.

But there was no way to get around the fact that Shank had changed visibly. He was less talkative than ever. He didn't seem to have any time for casual conversation. He rarely hung around the pad, rarely went out with them during the evenings. A few nights back a whole mob of them headed out around midnight, caught a late show in Times Square, then bought a few bottles of wine and went to Central Park. They stayed there all night long, singing at the top of their lungs, balling on occasion, making a major scene. But Shank hadn't wanted to come along. He had said he had things to do. But what kind of things? And how come he never talked about them?

A problem. But Joe Milani knew how to deal with problems. He had carefully cultivated a method over the days and weeks and months.

He simply ignored the problem.

From a pocket he took a paper-bound copy of Henry Miller's *Sexus* that somebody had carefully smuggled in on a return trip from Europe. He opened it to an intriguing passage, began to read, and forgot completely the changes in Anita and Shank.

After Anita left Joe she did more or less as she had told him she would. She bought the paper cup of Italian ice from the man with the wagon on Thompson Street. Then she walked east on Fourth Street, stopping at a few stores along the way to shop. She angled up First Avenue to Saint Marks Place and the apartment, where she unpacked what she had bought.

She put the kettle on the stove, filled it with water, put the rice into it. She let the rice boil for a while, then started to add the mussels and the chopped-up eel. She dropped other ingredients into the pot—some left-over chicken, two crabs, and miscellaneous seafood. Then she covered the pot, wondering if it were all right to watch it. A watched pot, they said, never boiled. That seemed physically illogical. Did watched pots boil? Did pot burn when you watched it? Many things to think about.

She sat down on the edge of the bed and tried to concentrate. She picked up a book and tried to read. Unable to concentrate, she gave up, tossing the book carelessly on the other bed. She stared across the room, waiting for something. For dinner to cook. For something, damn it.

She was sitting on the bed when Shank entered. Anita did not greet him, nor did Shank greet her. He walked to the stove, lifted the lid off the pot and sniffed like a comic-strip husband. He sauntered to his bed, picked up the book she had tossed there and looked through it. He threw it on the floor.

Then he turned his gaze on her. She felt there was something obscene in his expression. He kept staring at her till she flushed and turned away. When she looked back he was still staring at her in precisely the same way. She wanted to tell him to stop it but she did not know what to say. She wished again he would go away, so she and Joe could live alone. She would get a job—

it would be worth it if she and Joe could have a place of their own.

Shank still stared at her.

She returned his glance now. She searched his eyes, trying to figure out what was hidden there.

Then he told her.

"Strip," he said.

Her eyes widened.

"Strip. Get your clothes off and get 'em off fast. Strip!"

"What are you—"

His dead eyes blazed in his pale face. His mouth was smiling terribly. His voice was flat and deadly.

"I am going to do what I please with you. And you don't have a thing to say about it. Nothing. What I do to you is up to me. So get those clothes off fast."

"You're crazy!"

His hand slipped into his pocket and reappeared with a knife. She watched in morbid fascination as his fingers curled around the handle of the knife. He pressed the catch and the blade snickered out. She stared at it, watched light glinting on the carefully polished face of the blade that appeared to be very sharp.

"Strip," he repeated.

She was numb.

"You've got a choice," he told her. "You can take your clothes off or I can cut 'em off. It's up to you. I don't care one way or the other."

"Joe," she said. "Any minute. He's coming home. He's coming and—"

He turned and locked the door. "Thanks for putting me wise," he said. "Now the clothes. I'll cut 'em off of you if I have to. And I'll cut you up while I'm at it."

He was telling the truth, he would make good his threat if he had to. And there was nothing for her to do... Finally, when she kicked off her tennis shoes, she was naked. Now, his eyes were worse than ever. She felt as if she had taken off her skin and he was staring at her insides.

Shank approached the girl and held out the knife. She stared at the blade as a bird would at a snake. Then, after a long moment, she tried to move away. But the bed was behind her and the distance between them remained the same.

"Don't move," he advised her. "Not yet. You could get hurt. And Joe might not like you after I got through."

He was insane, Anita knew. He would kill her. She wanted to scream but she was too scared.

"Now undress me," Shank said.

When she hesitated, he repeated the command and backed it up by touching the knife to her and raising a tiny bead of blood.

Anita undressed him. His grin widened and his eyes became steadily more insane. She was terrified.

Then, casually, he folded up the knife and tossed it on his bed. He did this without taking his eyes from her. Then, as if he had all the time in the world, he drove his fist into the pit of her stomach. She clutched her stomach in agony, trying to hold back the pain. Tears came to her eyes and spilled over.

Then he slapped her across the face with all his force. The pain was like a knife. Her body began to tremble.

Then Shank began to curse her. He used language more obscene than anything she had ever heard. He cursed her intently and she listened to the words he spoke with her eyes wide and her heart beating violently.

Then he began to hit her again. Finally, he shoved her down to the bed and then it began.

It was long and bad and very painful. He seemed more concerned with hurting her than anything else. She lay inert, the pain washing over her in high and resonant waves. She lay there, on the bed she shared with Joe, while Shank made vile and brutal and horrible love to her.

Later, when her pain had subsided and she was dressed once more, Shank gripped her by the shoulders and spun her around to face him. She tried to turn away but he had her vised.

"You won't tell him," he said.

"I won't?"

He shook his head. "You won't tell him. You don't want to. You think you do but you're wrong."

"Why?"

He grinned. "Three things could happen," he said. "He could play protective male. He could decide to punish me for taking advantage of his poor, defenseless woman. And that would be a mistake. Because then I'd have to take care of myself. Have to protect myself, like any average all-American boy. And he's bigger than I am. Which means I'd have to make it closer. The knife. I'd have to cut old Joe a little."

He wasn't human, Anita thought. No human being could act as he did and talk as he did. Joe was his friend and she was Joe's girl, yet he could beat her and rape her and talk about knifing Joe as if it were the most natural thing in the world.

"Or he could decide you led me on. That's one way. He'd figure it was your fault and get mad at you. He'd beat you for dust, little girl. And you don't want that. Hell, one beating a day is plenty for you. Right?"

That wouldn't happen, she told herself. Joe would never do that. Never.

"Or one other thing. He wouldn't do anything. He'd just shrug it off and forget about it. Pretend you were jiving him or something, or else say it was between you and me and he didn't give a damn. And that would shake you up, little girl. Shake you six ways and home again."

"He wouldn't," she said.

"Naw," he drawled. "Not old Joe. That's what you want to think. You wouldn't want to find out he doesn't care more for you than he does for a used fish. And that's the big reason why you won't tell him. You dig the whole message? Any way you lose. Joe gets cut or you get hurt or Joe just doesn't give a damn. Three ways to lose and no ways to win. You know what? I think you'll keep that little mouth of yours sewed up nice and tight."

"You're a bastard, Shank."

He threw back his head and laughed. "That the best you can do? You can call me worse than that. Go ahead —talk a big streak."

She called him a foul name and he laughed harder. She swore up and down at him and he laughed until tears rolled down his cheeks.

"You're sick," Anita said. "You think pain is fun."

"If it's not my pain."

"You're sick."

He was laughing. "And you're fun. Lots of fun. And you're not going to say a word to Joe. You understand?"

Shank walked to the stove and lifted the lid. "Paella again," he said. "I can live without it."

"I can live without your company."

He laughed again. "I think I'll pass up your paella," he told her. "Catch a bite out somewhere. Give my regards to your man, Anita."

He laughed again, louder, and he was gone. She shut the door after him, sank on the bed, and cried.

When she stopped crying she thought she would tell Joe, and they would leave Shank. Why shouldn't she tell Joe? Shank's reasons were nonsense. They made no sense at all, and they were just an argument because he was afraid of what would happen if she did tell Joe.

She told herself that again and again.

But, when Joe came home, she acted as if nothing were wrong. All through dinner—the paella was delicious, although she hardly managed to taste it—she told herself she would tell Joe later, in a little while, later in the evening, after dinner.

But she did not tell him.

They stayed home that night and Shank did not show. They stayed home, and when Joe suggested smoking some pot she made no objection at all. She got very high.

But still she did not mention anything to Joe about what Shank had done.

Joe wanted to make love to her. But after what she'd been through, that was out of the question.

Anita lay awake for hours after they had gone to bed. Her brain reeled in circles and the sun was coming up before her mind finally blanked out and she drifted off to a hectic sleep.

9

"Let's move," she said to Joe.

"Solid. Where to? Want to fall up to 42nd Street and catch a movie?"

On this Thursday afternoon a hot sun shone high in the sky. Anita and Joe were home by themselves. Some two weeks had passed since Shank had cruelly assaulted the girl, and she had said nothing to Joe about it.

"That's not what I mean," Anita said.

"No?"

"I mean move out," Anita said. "Out of here."

"The apartment?"

"Let's get an apartment of our own," she said. "Just the two of us. Away from Shank."

He thought that one over. "Got any idea what we would use for bread?"

"I could get a job."

"Yeah," he said. "You mean I could get a job. That's the bit, isn't it? Go out and work, Joey. Go support me, Joey."

"I didn't say that."

"But you meant it. You didn't have to say it, baby. You meant it."

She started to deny it but stopped. She had not

meant it, not just then, but saying so would only be begging the question. The idea that he could certainly put in a few hours a day working had been in the back of her mind for quite a while. After all, it wasn't as though he did anything else. Some people could use writing or painting as an excuse. But not Joe. He did nothing, nothing at all.

"You want me to work," he said. "That's what you want, isn't it?"

"It wouldn't kill you."

He sighed. "You remember what you said once? About being a leopard and you couldn't change your spots?"

She remembered.

"You hit it, girl. Oh, you hit it on the top. Those spots of yours are permanent features, all right. You're the same little girl I found in The Palermo. You know that? The same little girl who lived in Harlem with Grandma and went out with that engineering wop Ray Somebody. You want the same damned thing you always wanted. You want security and heavy furniture and charge accounts. You want—"

"Did I say that? All I said was I wanted an apartment where we could be by ourselves! I said I'd get a job. Not you! I—"

A bitter laugh. "Uh-huh. Now it's an apartment. Then it'll be, *Joe, honey, we're living together so why don't we get married, it'll make things easier, why not.* The whole routine with a lot of yapping until you wind up with a ring on your finger. Then you'll want a kid, and then a house, a little split-level paradise out in the suburbs, and—"

"Stop that!"

He stopped.

Her eyes blazed. "Now you listen to me," Anita said. "Now you just turn it off for a minute and listen to me. All I want is for us to be alone. A-l-o-n-e. Alone, just us, no wedding ring, no house in hell, no nothing, no kid, no nothing, damn you to hell!" Her voice got louder and louder until, when she hit the last word, she was screaming. He stared at her, not believing what he was seeing or hearing.

"You listen," she went on. "You just shut that mouth of yours and you listen. Nobody's trying to run you. Nobody wants to own you. Own you! I wouldn't take you in marriage if you crawled. I'll live with you, I'm no good, you're no good, I'm a slut and you're a pig and I live with you. But marriage? You should live so long. You should positively live so long."

Joe had never seen her like this before. He was lost. It made no sense.

"Just to be alone," she said. "So we can live like people instead of animals. Not luxury. I wouldn't care if the place were worse than this. How that could happen I don't know, this place is for pigs, but it wouldn't matter. Just so we could live alone without the rest of the world in our living room, without that rat friend of yours here, without—"

She stopped. She took a breath. She found a cigarette and lit it and inhaled deeply.

"You think it over, Joe. You think about it. Because
it doesn't have to be that way. I can get the same job
either way, Joe. Either if we get our own apartment or
if I get my own apartment, and don't think I won't. You
think I'm trying to own you? I'll walk right out on you,
Joe. I can do it. It's up to you. I leave with you or without you but I will be damned if I'll go on living here."

She walked to the door. "I'll be back in an hour or
so," she said. "You make up your mind."

And she stormed out and slammed the door. He sat
there, his eyes on the door, and he thought about everything she had said and the way she had said it.

He was still sitting there when Shank came in.

"Shank," Joe said. "Got to talk to you."

"Yeah?"

"I got a problem, Shank."

"Bread?"

"No. Yes. I don't know."

"So talk."

"Anita and I are going to split."

"Leaving town?"

He shook his head. "Not that. To a pad of our own.
She wants to. You know how chicks get. They need
privacy."

"I get it."

"Which means I'll need money. I don't know how
I'm going to swing it. Like, you've been paying the tab

for a long time. Now I've got to pick up my own end of it. Anita says she'll get a job but that's no good. We couldn't make it that way. Which means, I'll have to find a gig."

"You think so?" Shank said flatly.

Joe shrugged. "Why not? Maybe something around the area, you know, because I have no eyes to put on a suit every morning. Clerking in a Village shop, waiting tables in a coffee house, something like that. I ought to be able to find a gig without sweating."

"Finding is easy. Holding is harder."

"I don't read you, man."

Shank lit a cigarette and talked through the smoke. "You really think you could hold a job? You think you could get up every morning and go to work no matter how dragged you felt?"

Joe was silent.

"Work," Shank said. "A nice draggy routine, one day after the other. You could ball it up on the weekend, man. No work for two whole days. And a hot dollar an hour would give you forty bucks to play around with. Man, you could really move on that sort of bread."

"What else is there?" Joe turned away. "That's just it, man. Either way I lose. I ought to be able to hold a job. I mean, there's a lot of pretty stupid cats working their eight hours a day with no trouble. So—"

"Maybe that's what makes them stupid."

Joe looked up.

"You want a job?" Shank grinned. "I'll give you a

job, baby. Sales work. You pick your own hours and you make all the bread you want. Get dragged and you take the day off. Get hungry and you work overtime. No sweat, not anywhere up or down the line. I'll give you a job if you're hungry. But don't go square on me. Don't clerk in a shop or wait tables in a coffee joint. If you want to work you might as well make it pay."

"You mean selling."

"What else?"

"Selling pot," Joe said. "I would have asked you. I didn't think you had enough trade to pass around."

Shank's smile spread.

"Selling pot," Joe repeated. "That's one easy circuit. Anita might not go for it. She's funny about that. But she'll learn. It's good bread and it's easy. You sure you'll cut me in on it?"

"Sure. But you're not clear on it."

"What do you mean?"

"I mean it's not pot."

"No? You branching out? Selling peyote, bennies, that type of stuff? I didn't know there was that kind of bread in it. Peyote and bennies are almost legal."

"Not peyote," Shank said. "Not benzedrine, not goof balls, not dexies. Something else."

He took Joe by the arm. "Come here," he said, leading him to the dresser. He pulled open the drawer, took out a small cardboard box, opened it.

Joe stared.

"Heroin," Shank said.

"That's evil stuff, Shank. I don't want to fool around with it."

"Who fools? I don't fool, man. I sell. A king-size difference. My customers like me. Everybody likes me. No sweat and no bother. You know the mark-up on this stuff? Fifty, seventy-five percent. Nice big margin. Can't lose, man."

"You can go to jail."

"They give tickets for jaywalking, baby. I still cross in the middle of the block. You can't swing with all the laws, Joe. You got to play it the way it has to be played. It's the only way."

Shank pursed his lips. It amazed him the way he always felt years older than Joe although chronologically it was the other way around. Now, I'm hiring Joe as a salesman after having ceremoniously raped Joe's woman not too long ago. Shank was getting a special kick.

"I can understand it," Shank said. "I been selling hard stuff since the Mau-Mau took his fall. My new connection put me wise to it. I was bugged at first. Nervous. Everybody on the street looked like law to me, every shadow a detective with a big gold badge and a cannon in his holster. You get used to it. The money is very tall and the customers come to you instead of the other way around. You get used to it and you get to like it. A man has a pocket load of horse and he never starves, Joe. Money in the bank. Think about it."

Joe picked up one of the capsules, held it between his thumb and forefinger. Anita wouldn't like his handling horse, he was certain. It was nothing they had ever talked about, but it was one of those things she was against, automatically.

But he also knew Shank was right about a job being no good for Joe. And Anita and he couldn't move out on Shank unless they had money. And they had to move out or Anita would move on her own.

Why not let her move and forget it? He wondered about that and couldn't come up with anything definite. In a number of ways the chick was an utter drag. No doubt about it—she was holding on, hanging on, wanting to change him, to grab him by the neck until he turned into a husband. But that was natural. She was a chick and chicks were like that. It was a question only of who would get there first, whether he could change her before she changed him. She was already very different from the innocent little virgin who had traipsed down to the Village to peer at the funny people. And she would change some more.

But now it was Joe's turn to make a concession. He and the girl would find an apartment. And he would sell for Shank. He could be cool about it. The police would never catch him.

"I'm in," he said finally.

"Solid. We go out together tomorrow. I'll hit you with a customer or two. Introduce you. Then you take the junk from me and sell it to them and we work out a split. I figure a straight split of fifty-fifty on the profits is straight enough. How about you?"

"Whatever you say."

"You'll make a few bills a week once you get going. Five or six times what they would pay you for clerking in a shop somewhere. It's good money. Then you and the chick can take your own apartment. Hell, on that kind of bread you can take a good apartment. Maybe something in the West Village. Or uptown. Anywhere. Furnish it up nice. She would like that."

"She probably would."

"Women are that way," Shank said. "You probably worry about her not liking this gig. Well, she won't. I can tell you that right now."

"I know."

"But she'll get used to it. She likes certain things. A nice pad, good furniture, a fridge full of food, a little money to blow on clothes. Give her all that and she'll forget where the bread comes from. It's amazing the way a chick can forget what she wants to forget."

"I suppose so."

"Money," Shank said. "You know what I been doing? Been playing it cool, Joe. Got a bank account. Bank way uptown, another name on the account. The extra money goes there. Every week some more money goes in the account. In a couple of years I get out. Empty the account, put the dough in a money belt and disappear. I wind up in another town in another part of the country. Good clothes, lots of money. A stranger with plenty of money and a lot on the ball. I find my own place. Buy a club, maybe. Something like that. A fresh start with no questions and nobody who knows who I am. A new name and a new world. All ready to roll for me."

"I didn't know that. I thought you spent everything."

"You thought wrong."

"You got all the angles working for you," Joe said. "I don't know if I'll do it that way. Just make the money and spend it. Take it easy."

"You make your own life," Shank said thoughtfully. "It's up to you. People get what they want. That's how it goes, nine times out of ten."

Anita was up in Harlem. She had taken the train there when she had left Joe; for perhaps an hour she had walked familiar streets and had seen familiar people. She had talked to some, for a moment or two, until there had been the mutual feeling of estrangement.

Now, sadly, Anita returned to the subway station. Harlem was another world now, the girl could not escape concluding. She no longer knew the people living there. She had become a part and parcel of Saint Marks Place. She lived with Joe and Shank.

And you could never go back, she ruefully reflected. Not in a million years. You couldn't reset the clock.

Back on the train, back to Saint Marks Place, back to Joe. But certain things would have to change, Anita determined. She and Joe would have to secure an apartment of their own. Either that or, by God, she would move to a furnished room and live her own life. She wanted Joe, needed Joe, maybe loved Joe. But enough was enough and she had definitely, certainly, positively had more than enough. Enough of Shank, enough of the apartment on Saint Marks Place, enough of aimless living. There had to be another way to find yourself. You could find yourself without losing both yourself and the world in the process.

The train released her and in a few minutes she found herself back in the apartment. Joe and Shank were waiting for her.

"Something to tell you," Joe said. "Got a job. We can have our own place now."

At first Anita did not believe him. Then the news soaked in and her lips turned up in an automatic smile. Their own place, she exulted. Joe with a job. Their own life, and it could be a good life now, a clean life.

"What kind of a job?" she asked brightly.

"Sales work."

Something rang false to the girl. "What kind of sales work?" she wanted to know. And at the same time she did not want to know, because she already felt she knew the answer. And it was the wrong answer.

But Joe told her.

"Selling what Shank sells," he said.

And, when she turned white, not even realizing he was saying, cryptically, he would be selling not pot but heroin, Joe tried to explain.

"Just for a little while," he said. "Just until we get our heads above water. It's safe, baby, it's safe and it's easy and it's good bread. We can get a nice pad in a good neighborhood and live decent. And as soon as we get a little bit ahead I'll look for a good job, an honest one, and we'll be moving. I mean it, Anita."

Half of her mind realized he was lying. He would keep the easy money, the easy life. But the other half of her mind said she herself would turn his lie into truth, and he would change because of her. And then he would get that good job, that honest job, and it would all have been worth it. Their life would be good. "I'll start tomorrow," he said. "And tomorrow you go and look for an apartment. A decent one. Go as high as two hundred a month if you want. And unfurnished if you want. We'll buy furniture. A little at a time, not too expensive, but decent furniture. We'll fix the place up nice and we'll live in it."

A good apartment, Anita listened to her racing thoughts. That would be nice. A good apartment with good furniture in a good neighborhood. More than she had expected. And for two hundred dollars a month they could afford a nice place.

"Then we'll start to roll," he said, getting carried away now, half believing it himself. "We'll get money ahead and I'll get a good job. Maybe with a publishing house or an advertising agency. Something a little creative so I don't go out of my mind. And we'll live good, honey. Really live good. We don't have to be rich. Just so we aren't starving and we don't live like pigs."

His words intoxicated her and her head began to swim. The vision was perfect, so she put her arms around him, ashamed of herself for having walked out on him before, ashamed for having yelled at him and ashamed for having come so close to hating him. She kissed him.

Shank abruptly left without being asked. And then Joe stripped the girl while her skin tingled in anticipation. And then he touched her, curve for curve, swell for swell, till they tumbled to the bed and their bodies hounded each other.

It was very good.

The sun and the moon and the stars. The earth trembling, rocking, jolting.

They moved frantically until they trapped each other in a sweaty fever-lock.

Good.

Very good.

And, when the world exploded, Anita knew—with earth-shaking certainty—that at last everything was going to be all right.

But she was wrong.

The next day developed according to plan.

Shank arose early to go to his bank on Fifth Avenue where he deposited money in his savings account. Then he returned to the apartment and woke Joe.

In the course of the day Shank took Joe to three of the former's customers. "This is Joe," he told each one. "He's my man. From now on you cop from him."

And the customers digested this information and filed it away in junkie minds.

Anita spent the day hunting a suitable apartment. She bought the *New York Times* and checked out the ads. Two apartments she examined were suitable. One, located in the Village, a two-room, second-floor apartment on Bank Street, rented for a hundred and sixty. The other rented for one-forty, a two-room, first-floor place on East 19th Street near Gramercy Park. The building was immaculate, the apartment rent-controlled, and Anita preferred it.

But she did not rent either apartment. Instead, she decided to discuss the matter with Joe. Maybe he would prefer one location to another, or one apartment to another. After all, he had a right to participate in the decision since they were renting the apartment together.

She trotted back to Saint Marks Place and started dinner. Shank and Joe appeared a few minutes before dinner was ready. They talked about what they had done that afternoon and Anita thought hysterically of this insane domestic scene. Her man had a new job. He sold marijuana. And now she was cooking for him and his—his boss, for the love of God.

Dinner was veal chops. Veal chops and mashed

potatoes and green peas. She served them all and they sat down to eat. Dinner for the boss. A strange tableau.

She described the two apartments to Joe, told him about both places. "I think I liked the one in Gramercy a little better," she said. "It's smaller but there's only the two of us. And it's a nice place."

"Sounds good," Joe said.

"The Bank Street place is nice, too. But I'm a little sick of the Village. And I didn't like the building there as much. The rent is higher and you don't get as much for your money."

"Whatever you want," he said. "It's up to you. Just so we get a nice pad."

The veal chops were good, the potatoes smooth, the peas young and sweet. They finished and she carried the plates to the sink and ran water on them.

The water was still running when the door was kicked open.

The man who had kicked it open was Detective First Grade Peter J. Samuelson, Narcotics Bureau.

He had a gun in his hand.

10

The detective said: "You never learn. You have to push your luck. You have to lean until you fall. Now you fall."

The running water in the sink was very loud. Anita took tentative steps toward Joe, but an unmistakable motion from Samuelson halted her.

"A long fall," the detective said. "A long, long fall. Possession with intent. Rather obvious intent. You had a chance last time and you blew it, you damned fool," he addressed the words to Shank.

What happened next occurred in slow motion. Shank unwound like a cobra. He stood up and grabbed Anita in one fluid movement. Then Anita was being propelled swiftly at Detective Samuelson. His gun was pointed between her breasts but he did not fire it.

And Shank moved behind her. He moved with the grace of a dancer. His legs thrust him forward while his hand dipped in his pocket and brought out his knife. The knife danced in his hand and the blade leaped out, alert.

Anita's softness bounced into the detective. She fell away, limp, and Shank's knife bit, cobralike, into the man with the gun. Slow motion. The knife sneaking between ribs, ripping upward. The gun, still unfired, dropping from limp fingers and clattering inanely on the bare floor.

The detective's hard body losing its hardness. A hand clutching at the hole the knife had made, the man trying to hold life in place. The knife withdrawn, and flowers of ruby blood blossoming from a hole in a chest.

A body falling slowly, crumpling, folding to the floor. A suppressed scream from Anita, a gasp from Joe.

Then quietude, except for the running water slapping at the dirty dishes in the sink.

A tragicomedy in one act, a quick act. A gun on the floor, unfired. The knife dripping the detective's blood.

The detective on the floor.

Dead.

The water in the sink was still running.

Anita spoke first. Her voice was a loud whisper. "You killed him. Oh, God, God in heaven, you killed him. He's dead and you killed him."

"I had to."

"Had to? A year and a day for possession of pot. That's what you would have gotten. Now you'll get the electric chair. Murder. Murder in the first degree. The electric chair. Holy mother of God!"

Shank's brain was swimming. This was what it felt like, he thought. This is how killing felt. A strange feeling of power combined with the damnedest emptiness. A funny sort of a feeling.

"A year and a day. That's what they would have given you. Possession of pot," Anita echoed herself fatuously.

Shank grabbed her roughly by the arm. "Possession of pot," he snapped. "You think that's what it is, huh? You think that's the whole ball game. You know all the answers, don't you? You think you know just what your man sells, baby. You're all mixed up. All wrong."

Then he opened the dresser drawer, took out the little box. He opened it and showed her the capsules of heroin and smiled when she drew in her breath sharply.

"God!"

"A year and a day," Shank said savagely. "Try ten years. Try fifteen or twenty. And not just for me. For me and for your man, Joe. For both of us with a little bit thrown in for you just for being here. How would you like to do a few years?"

"Murder," she said, numb. "Heroin. God in heaven."

Joe sat and stared. He, too, was numb, unable to think straight. It had happened so quickly while he simply sat and watched. The detective, the gun, the knife. Death, so quick. He felt left out now. But he stood up. He walked to Anita, put an arm around her. He looked at Shank.

"What do we do now?"

"We move," Shank said. "We get out of town. What else can we do?"

"We have to run?"

Shank shook his head impatiently. "The cop let the world know where he was. If he doesn't call in within an hour they'll come looking for him. Even if we ditch the body it won't do us any good. They'll shake us down until they break us. They'll nail us to fourteen different crosses. They'll hang us, put us in the chair, whatever they do. We'll die."

"You'll die," Anita told him, "You killed him. We didn't do it."

"Read another law book. You're guilty, too, sweetheart. Possession with intent to sell is a felony. We all possessed with intent. And if somebody kills in the commission of a felony, it's murder one. The detective was killed and we were all here. We all get the chair."

"But—" Joe began.

"So we run," Shank said. "We got two hours to get out of town. Breeze to Grand Central and take the first train out. Get out far and fast. They won't know where to look. We leave the state and keep going and they call it unsolved. We leave New York and we stay living. Otherwise we die. I don't want to die."

"You can go," she said. "Joe and I don't have to go. They're not after us. They're after you. We didn't do anything and we don't have to run with you."

"They'll catch you," Shank said. "They'll pick you up and they'll squeeze you. They'll ask you where I went."

"Don't tell us. Then we won't be able to tell them anything because we won't know."

"They'll call you accessories," Shank said. "They'll put you in jail."

"No—"

"You got no choice. We hang together or we hang separately. You've got to come with me."

Joe was nodding. "He's right," he said. "But not all the way. I've got to go with him, Anita."

"No you don't. No—"

"I've got to," Joe said again. "But you don't. They don't know anything about you. You can disappear. Go back to Harlem. Forget about us. We'll run and we'll get away but you can go on living. The fuzz doesn't know who you are. You can forget us and live your own life."

Shank nodded. "I'll buy it," he said. "She could get away. But Joe and I have to run."

Anita hesitated only for a moment. She knew she was making the wrong decision but she knew also it was the only decision she could possibly make. She was committed. She shared their guilt in her own small way. And she and Joe were thrust together. She could not walk away from him. Not now, not ever.

"I'll come with you," she said.

"You don't have to."

"I have to. I have to, now, forever. I'll come with you, I will."

"No time to pack," Shank was saying. "We take what we can carry. We head first for Buffalo. It's a big junk town. I can sell there. We can get some money together."

They were short on money. Shank had fifty dollars in cash and the cop's wallet yielded another twenty-five. Joe had a few dollars, Anita a few more. Enough to get them to Buffalo and pay for a hotel room, maybe a meal. Nothing more.

"All that money in the bank," Shank said. "All that goddamn money and the bank doesn't open until Monday. Can't risk it. Can't stay around. They'll tip to us by then. And they won't let up. The police take care of their own. Kill a cop and they turn the town inside-out looking for you. Someday I'll come back, clean out that bank account. Not now."

Shank and Joe stuffed the cop's hard body into the closet. They covered the bloodstains with newspapers. "They'll find him," Shank said. "Maybe this will keep them an extra hour. Maybe two hours. Every minute helps."

Curiously, Anita remembered to turn off the water running in the sink, thinking as she did so that the water would have washed nothing away, anyhow. The scum on the dirty dishes was very thick.

They took a cab to Grand Central. Their timing was fortunate. A train left for Buffalo at 8:02 and they were on it. Shank had his knife in one pocket and the cop's gun in the other. Joe was carrying the heroin. There was a lot of it—Shank had connected recently with Basil.

"We'll sell it in Buffalo," he said. "Lay over a few

days, sell what we can, then head west. Buy a car. It's safer by car. Trains make me nervous."

The train stopped at Albany. A porter rolled through a sandwich cart. Shank bought three sandwiches and he, Joe and Anita wolfed them down without tasting them. The train started up again and sped west.

"Chicago," Shank said. "We can hole up in Chicago. I know a cat from the coast, he's in Chicago. An old friend. We can connect with him, hide out there. Set ourselves up, get rolling again. Just so we get out of the state. New York's going to be too hot."

Utica. Syracuse.

Joe wondered what was going to happen. It was bad now, very bad. It could only get worse. A man was stuck in a closet with a hole in his chest and they had put him there.

You could defend a lot of things, rationalize a lot of actions. You could defend smoking, defend selling. Somebody had to sell it, Joe's mind ticked off the thoughts.

Murder was different.

Run, he thought. Run all you want. But where can you hide? How far can you run before they catch you?

Joe looked at Anita and wondered why she had tagged along. He was somehow a little glad she was with them. He needed her. He took her hand now and held it. If only that cop had stayed away. He and Anita would have had their own place. And finally he would be money ahead and he could get a job and everything would be all right, good and clean and proper.

Not running.

Not looking for a place to hide.

Why had she come along? Of the three, she alone was safe. She alone could go home, back to Harlem, back to something approaching sanity. She could stay away from police, she could be safe. Nobody knew her. Nobody was looking for her.

And yet she had chosen to be with him. Now she was breaking the laws. Accessory to and after the fact. Guilty, now.

Why?

Rochester. Batavia.

Anita sat in her seat and tried to sleep but could not. She wondered when she would be able to sleep again. Some time, maybe.

Joe was holding her hand, squeezing it. She wanted to squeeze back but she was still numb and she could not move. She felt as if she were not really alive. Everything was a dream. A big bad dream. A nightmare she was somehow living her way through. A bad nightmare that would have a dismal ending.

They were running. First to Buffalo. Then to Chicago, then to somewhere else. She wondered when they would be able to stop running. Never, she decided. They would run until they dropped, run until they were caught and tried and electrocuted. She wondered if she would be killed with the others. She wondered if it made any difference, if anything made any difference any more.

Probably not.

She lit a cigarette from the butt of another and the smoke scratched her throat and clouded her lungs. She coughed out a cloud of smoke and her head swam. Nothing mattered any more. Nothing would ever matter. She and Joe were together, they would run together, they would be caught together, they would die together. Nothing mattered. Nothing would ever matter.

Buffalo.

The train jolted to a stop and they stood up together and walked out of it.

Buffalo was gray in the morning. Anita, Joe and Shank left the railroad station and took a taxi to a dilapidated hotel on Clinton Street where the desk clerk asked no questions. They paid ten dollars in advance and the clerk gave them a room on the third floor whose window opened out on an air shaft. The room was dirty, the two beds unmade.

"It's quiet," Shank said. "And we won't be here long. A day, two days. Then we clear out and head west. We leave this town behind us. A bad town to begin with. And in the wrong state—for us. There are forty-nine other states. We'll do better in any one of them. Not New York."

He took the heroin from Joe, put it in the dresser drawer. "You stay here," he said. "The two of you, stay in the room, keep it quiet. I'll be back in an hour, two hours. Wait for me."

He went out and left them alone.

For several minutes they sat by themselves and said nothing. Then Joe broke the silence.

"You didn't have to come," he said.

"I know."

"Why?"

"I don't know. I guess I had to be with you. I don't know why."

"You were nuts to come. I don't know how we're going to get away."

She said nothing.

"But I'm glad you came," he went on. "I'm selfish, but I'm glad you came. I would go nuts without you. I need you, Anita."

She looked at him.

"Anita," he said. "I love you, Anita."

She went to him and sat on the bed with him. He put his arms around her, slowly, tentatively, and their mouths came together and they kissed. A long kiss. A good kiss, a kiss saying many things.

"We have to stay together. We need each other, Anita. And some day we'll get out of this. Out all the way. It'll be the two of us forever."

"I hope so, Joe."

"It will. It will, honey. I love you, honey, I love you and I need you and—"

It happened like a dream. There was no need to talk any more. They were lost in their overwhelming need, a need that could only be satisfied through the merging of flesh with flesh, body with body, soul with soul. They undressed automatically and they came together with no preceding love-play, no kisses, no caresses. His flesh claimed her and they joined in a dreamlike version of reality, bodies seeking, hearts pounding, minds clouded with love.

When it was finished they lay in each other's arms, holding themselves together, trying to right their lives with the sudden enormity of their love for each other. In the peak of passion they had managed to lose the horror of reality, the true nature of their situation. Now, as they basked in the glow of after-love, that horror filtered through to them once again.

But they had each other, and somehow this lessened the horror. As long as they were together they could survive it.

Finally, they slept…

Shank let them sleep. He let himself into the hotel room, walked to the dresser and removed the capsules of heroin from the drawer. He seated himself at the table and took out the things he had purchased.

Carefully he opened each capsule and diluted it with the milk sugar he had bought. He converted the thirty capsules into ninety capsules, each one-third as strong as the original ones had been. His investment was quickly tripled. He had three times the capital he had started with.

Of course, each capsule was now worth one-third of what it had originally been worth. It was, in the junkie's jargon, beat stuff. But the buyers did not have to know this. They would discover this only when they would use the capsules and derive a lesser kick from them than what they had been accustomed to. By that time Shank and Joe and Anita would be on their way, and goodbye Buffalo.

It was a bad town, anyway. A dull gray town. Shank would connect now, and sell the ninety capsules as quickly as possible, and then the three would blow town. So long, Buffalo. Later for you, suckers.

He slipped out of the room without waking Joe and Anita and took the heroin to the customers.

They were awake when he returned. "Come on," he said. "Let's move. We've got to get out of town."

"What's the matter?" Joe said.

"Nothing," he said. "No more horse. All sold."

"How?"

"Sold it for three bucks a cap," he said. "A good price. Junk comes high in Buffalo. I was selling for half price. The buyers were very hungry. I holed up in a little bar in the middle of Spadesville and the trade was fast and thick. Half a dozen customers and we were all out and the store was closed. So we have to scram in a hurry."

"Why the rush?"

Shank explained the customers would be ready to kill him in a very short time. He explained that he had sold one-third strength heroin for a heavy price, all things considered, and a lot of people would be mad at him when they would discover they had been taken.

"So we run," he explained. "I got better than two and a half bills. Ninety caps, bargain rate of three bucks a cap. We can buy a car. Not the best short in the world but one that will move for us. Let's go."

On the way to the used car lot Joe bought an evening paper. The Buffalo paper had the story on a back page. Detective First Grade Peter J. Samuelson was dead as a lox. The police were searching for his killers.

Shank bought a seven-year-old Chev for two hundred dollars. It was worth less than half of that but the dealer knew something was wrong. Shank had to pay his price, and did.

The car was a lemon. It rattled at fifty-five miles an hour. The brakes were in bad shape. The clutch could not work smoothly. The gears ground half the time.

But it would do.

Joe drove. He had no license but neither did Shank nor Anita. Joe knew how to drive so he drove. He took Route 20 out of town and headed for Cleveland.

Cleveland would be safe for a day or two. They could scrape together a little more money. Head for Chicago.

Anita sat next to him in the front seat. Shank slept in the back. Joe drove slowly and steadily. He could not have exceeded the speed limit if he had wanted to, and he did not want to. Not when he had no license. Not when the three were wanted for murder.

Murder.

They stopped twice on the way. They had hotdogs in Lodi and hamburgers in Ashtabula. Joe drove all the way until they were in Cleveland. He found a place to leave the car and they looked for a hotel.

They found one at 13th and Paine. It bore a startling resemblance to the one they had occupied in Buffalo. Again they paid in advance. Again the room was a mess.

Joe was tired from the drive and went to sleep at once. Anita stayed with Joe while Shank went out to find a beanery for a meal. On the way he stopped at a newsstand selling out-of-town papers, where he bought a copy of the *New York Times*.

It carried the story.

The cops knew too much. They had determined that two men and a girl had been involved in the murder. They had descriptions of Shank and Joe. They had lifted fingerprints from the apartment. They had one name—Shank Marsten. They did not have Joe's name, or at least it had not been released by the newspapers so far.

The police further figured the trio had left town; consequently, a state-wide alarm was out. There was a report the three had showed in Buffalo. Shank read that part and cursed quietly and methodically. He wondered how the cops had ascertained that. He wondered how much else they knew.

Shank ordered a chopped steak with home fries and a cup of coffee. The meat was good, the potatoes a little greasy, the coffee weak. He ate everything on his plate and drank two cups of coffee.

He tipped the waitress. He gave her a smile and she returned it. She was a pretty girl. Light red hair. And a good pair the white uniform could not hide. A nice rear end. He wondered if he could make a pass at her. He decided not to, even though she looked as if she would be fun in the sack. Too risky.

He smiled again and she gave him back such a good, wide, toothy smile he knew she would be flat on her back the minute he asked her. He wondered what she would say if she would find out he was a vicious killer. That was what the papers called him. A vicious killer.

The waitress would be scared green.

"I get off at one," she told him.

"I'll be back," he said. Let her think so if she wanted to, Shank thought. Let her wait—for a vicious killer.

He left the beanery and wandered back to the hotel. A vicious killer, he chuckled to himself. He rememberd how it had felt, killing the cop. A strange

feeling. Equal parts of power and emptiness. A funny
sensation.

Now the trio was running. Running fast and running scared. In a day or so the cops would know about
the car. It would have to be ditched, Shank knew.
Maybe trade it in for another one. Where would they
get the money?

A vicious killer. He did not feel very vicious. He
remembered the way he had moved in, using the girl
as a shield, his knife moving in on the cop. He remembered the funny feeling of power and emptiness.

He wondered if he would have to kill again, and how
it would feel a second time.

The trio stayed close to home. Two would remain in
the hotel room, sleeping or waiting, while the other
would prowl the gray streets of Cleveland. Shank
looked for people he knew, racket people, junk people.
He was on the make for some sort of a connection—
and came up with nothing.

And time bled them. The hotel took its cut and the
diners took their cut. And the money went—quickly,
too quickly, while the car sat alone on a quiet street as
the trio waited for the time to head for Chicago.

Each reacted in his own way. Shank was always
searching for a way, a chance, a shot in the endless
dark. He tried the bars in the Negro section where
horns wailed all night long and sleek dark women
wiggled their hips in open invitation. He tried the
waterfront, the lake shore, where bars overflowed with

dock workers and where the mouths of the whores were bloody with lipstick. He tried the waiting places—the bus station, the railroad terminal, the park.

He came up with nothing.

Joe retreated to a fantasy world. He spent his money on paperback books. He bought the books five or six at a time and took them back to the room. There he read one after another, letting the prose draw a curtain shutting out reality. When he spoke to Shank or to Anita his voice was loose and easy, flip and cool, an absolute denial of running and hiding. His fingers turned the pages of book after meaningless book, and his eyes vacantly scanned words to hurry on.

Anita turned into herself. But she could find neither salvation nor escape from reality. She, like Joe, spent the bulk of her time in the small room. But she did not read, although the many books Joe had discarded lay about her. Instead, she sat on the bed and stared at nothing. She spoke rarely, and then only in answer to a question from either Shank or Joe. She thought her own thoughts without attempting to share them. They were not happy thoughts. But they were hers, and she ran them again and again.

It was evening. Joe was lying on a bed, book in his hand, a western entitled *A Sound of Distant Drums,* by James Blue. Anita was sitting on the edge of the other bed and staring emptily across the room.

The door opened. It was Shank.

"We got to move," he said. He was holding a copy of

the *Cleveland Press* in one hand. He folded it and tossed it to the floor.

"They made the car," he said. "They got license, description, the works. They know we headed for Cleveland. We got to get out of here."

"We take the car, man?"

Shank shook his head, impatient with Joe. "They made the car, damn it. They maybe already found it. They maybe have it all staked out just waiting for us to come back. We don't touch the car. We don't go near that car. We get the first bus to Chicago and we leave this town far behind. That's what we do."

"Now?" Joe said.

Shank lit a cigarette. "Problem," he said. "A long problem."

"Go on."

"We're out of bread. Not starving. But we can't swing tickets to Chi."

"All that money from Buffalo—"

"The car," Shank reminded him. "And the hotel. And food. We're broke, man. Broke."

"What do we do?"

Shank considered. "Be ready to leave," he said. "You and the chick, be ready to leave in a hurry. I'll be back as soon as I can."

Joe nodded, thought for perhaps three seconds, then returned his attention to *A Sound of Distant Drums*. Anita remained motionless. They would be caught soon. Caught. And they could stop running, and they could stop hiding, and they could stop living.

And Shank went out, alone.

He could ditch them, Shank was thinking. He could leave them here, to rot.

There was enough money left for one ticket to Chicago, Shank considered. Not enough for three, not nearly enough. But enough to get Shank there. Then he would find Bunky, he would turn over the whole town until he found him, and then Bunky would turn Shank on to the Chicago scene and everything would be all right again. Shank would find himself a gig again, a pushing gig or a boosting gig or something where the money came quick and easy. And the heat would go down a little at a time until it was cool again. Then he would go back to New York and empty his savings account and head somewhere else with all that money and find the right place and the right ticket.

Joe and Anita could make out for themselves, Shank deliberated. Maybe they would be clear, maybe the cops wouldn't find them at all. They could stay alive. Anita could go out and hustle, turn a few tricks to keep Joe and herself eating regularly. Hell, the way it was the girl didn't do a damned thing. Just sat around on her duff and took up space. No reason why she couldn't turn a trick or two.

And Shank—Shank would be in Chi. Living free and clear and easy.

But he knew it wasn't going to happen that way. He crouched in the alley, waiting, and he knew he was not going to run out on them. He wasn't sure of his motives. He didn't need them. They were excess baggage. They couldn't think and they couldn't act.

And yet he couldn't ditch them.

He crouched in the alley and his fingers curled around the butt of the gun. The cop's gun. The cop was dead now and his gun was in Shank's hand. The gun was loaded all the way. The cop never had a chance to empty the gun, so now he was dead and Shank had the gun for himself.

Stupid cop, Shank thought. He should have shot the chick right off the bat, put a bullet in Anita, then stepped aside and let Shank have a slug in the face. But the cop was the chivalrous type. Wouldn't shoot a woman. Wasn't nice and proper. So the cop was dead and Shank was alive.

Shank kneeled in the alley. The ground was covered with gravel and it was uncomfortable. He wished somebody would come. He was getting a little edgy. The gun felt cold in his hand.

Maybe he could have sold the gun. A good piece was worth long bread to somebody who didn't have a permit. A piece that couldn't be traced. A nice safe piece. It could bring up to a hundred dollars, a long bill for a piece of metal with six bullets in it.

But no. Instead, he would use the gun. Who knew what it would bring?

He heard footsteps.

His muscles went tense. He leaned out of the alley-way, his eyes keen and aware. He saw a woman, her hair bound up in a babushka, her coat cheap cloth, her shoes worn. A pocketbook hanging from one arm. But what could there possibly be in the pocketbook—maybe a hot two dollars in change?

He let her pass and went on waiting.

Maybe he had picked the wrong place. What did he know about Cleveland? Shank felt doubts assail him. Maybe nobody ever walked around that street at night. Maybe people walked other streets. Maybe people did not walk at all in Cleveland at night. Maybe they all took cabs. Maybe they went to bed when the sun went down. Maybe—

More footsteps.

He peered out, cautiously. No good. Two kids, teen-agers. Fifteen, sixteen years old. Punk kids, lousy little two-bit punk kids walking home.

Shank retreated into the alley, acting on instinct. And they, halting at the alley, turned into it. One of the punks took something from the pocket of his black leather jacket. A cigarette? A match flared. One drew on the cigarette, then passed it to the other.

A waft of smoke found its way to Shank's nostrils. Pot. For the everloving motherjumping love of Jesus Christ, the little punks had to pick his alley to blow pot in. A whole city to turn on in and they had to pick his alley!

He raised the gun in his hand. He aimed carefully, holding the taller of the two kids in his sight. His finger was tense on the trigger.

Kill 'em. Blow their punk heads off—the desire raced through him.

He lowered the gun, trembling slightly. He waited, impatiently, while they finished the joint and discarded the roach in the alley. Then he waited until they walked away. He took up his former position and hoped somebody would come in a hurry. He couldn't wait much longer.

Hurry up, hurry up, come on, damn you to hell, come on. He cursed softly and listened to silence. He heard an automobile horn blocks away on another street. He waited and time crawled at an incredibly slow pace.

He stared at the cop's gun. A complex machine, he nodded to himself. You aimed it, you squeezed the trigger. That drew the hammer back and released it. The hammer slammed the end of the cartridge and detonated the powder charge. The force of the explosion propelled the bullet, the slug of lead, through the chamber and out of the muzzle of the gun into whatever object at which the gun had been aimed. A complex mechanism. Not like the knife, no mechanism at all. The knife was simply a sharpened steel blade you stabbed directly into a person. The knife was an extension of your arm, a kind of long, sharp hand.

He stared at the gun. He put his nose to the barrel

and smelled. The cop had cared for his gun. It had been oiled recently. It had a good machine-oil smell to it. And it hadn't been fired in a long time. There was no cordite smell.

Shank waited.

Then footsteps.

Again he leaned forward slowly, carefully. He saw the person approaching. Not a woman with a babushka. Not a pair of punk kids.

A man.

The man was about fifty. He had gray hair and he wore wire-rimmed glasses. He was slender, medium height. He could have been either a small storekeeper or an accountant.

He was the one.

When he passed the alley, Shank was behind him. Before the man took two more steps, the gun was in the small of his back.

"Stop," Shank said, very quietly.

The man stopped in his tracks.

"Now turn." Shank calmly issued the directions. "Now into the alley. That's the ticket. Keep walking. That's right. Now stop, and don't turn around."

The man seemed unafraid.

"You're making a mistake," he said.

Shank told him to shut up. "Your wallet," he said. "No tricks. Just take the wallet out and toss it over your shoulder."

The man's hand dipped gracefully into his inside

jacket pocket. The hand came out with a wallet.

"Toss it over here. Nice and easy. No tricks."

The wallet arched in the air. Shank caught it in his left hand. His right hand held the gun. The wallet was expensive pigskin worn smooth by years of use. He flipped it open. Not too much money. But enough.

"I don't begrudge you the money," the man said now. "But you're making a mistake. Embarking on a career of crime. Stop now, son. Before it's too late. You sound like a young fellow. You have a full life ahead of you."

"You know it all," Shank said.

"A full life," the man said. His voice was, if anything, too calm. "A man like me, I'm over the hill. I am what I am. I can't change myself. But you can be whatever you want to be, son. Don't be a criminal. It's no life for a young man like yourself. No life at all. Running and hiding. Bad."

The gun was warmer now. The steel was not so cold. Shank's hands had warmed the metal.

"A wonderful thing to be young," the man said. "Oh, these are bad times. No question about it. But a young fellow like you could find work. A good job. Chance for advancement. Not like me. Old man like me lands in a rut and stays in it. No choice for me. I'm over the hill. I'm at the end of my rope."

You don't know how true that is, Shank thought. How very true indeed.

"A fellow like you—"

That was all the old man said. Because Shank's finger tightened on the trigger and the gun was a living creature, alive and leaping in his hand. The first bullet entered the small of the man's back and he crumpled to the ground, all bent and twisted. The gun jumped. Shank lowered it and fired again. The second and third bullets smashed into the man's head and made a mess out of it. The fourth and fifth and sixth bullets made holes between the man's waist and back.

There was a moment when time stopped, when the world was suspended in the middle of the air. Like killing the cop, Shank remembered. All that power and all that emptiness. The tremendous noise of the gun—six noises grouped into one—all that power and all that emptiness.

God!

The worn pigskin wallet fitted into Shank's pocket. The gun—empty now, and useless—fell clattering to the ground. For a shadow of time, Shank stood poised in the alleyway, listening to the potent silence, waiting for something undefined.

Then he ran.

He raced out of the alley to the street, turned down the street and headed west as fast as he could go. He ran at top speed for three blocks without stopping, expecting the high-pitched squeal of police sirens, the whine of a bullet, the voice of a cop shouting, *Stop or I shoot, stop or I shoot,* the bullets whistling and hitting, piercing skin and flesh and bone.

Still there was nothing but silence. So Shank halted for a moment, finally, and then began walking more slowly, forcing himself to stay cool, calm and cool, cool and collected. He stopped by a mailbox and removed the money from the wallet. Enough to get them to Chicago and not much more. The man had not been rich. An old man, a poor old man. Dead.

The man had talked about youth. His whole life ahead of him. The future. Oh, the old man was wrong.

Dead wrong.

Run, Shank thought. Run, run, run. And you ran as fast as you could and you didn't get anywhere. The most you ever got to was the one pretty minute of power, the gun smoking and a man all broken and bloody and dead. And then you had to run some more, and God in heaven there was never a place to hide, never a pillow to rest your head on, never a hiding place, hiding place, place to rest. God!

Shank walked to the bus station. Because there was no time to return to the hotel for Anita and Joe, no time at all. Soon the dead man would be found in the alley. Maybe ten minutes of grace remained—maybe an hour, a day. The cops would run down Shank. They *could* trace the gun, trace it to the dead cop with the hole in his chest, trace it to Shank and Joe and Anita.

Cleveland was far too small. Too small to hide in, too small to stay in.

Run.

Run!

He ducked in a phone booth in the Greyhound station, dropped a dime in the slot. The man in the alley was dead. His wallet was in a mailbox. His money was in Shank's pocket. Run, damn you. Run like hell and where do you hide? Where?

He dialed the number of the hotel. The desk clerk answered, his voice thin, whiny.

"Room 304."

Joe picked up the phone. His hello was guarded, frightened. We're all afraid, Shank thought. Afraid and running, running scared. No way to do it.

"Greyhound station," Shank said. "Fast as you can. Don't waste any time."

Joe rang off without reply. Shank walked to the ticket counter where he obtained the information that a bus was leaving for Chicago in less than an hour. He bought three tickets one-way.

He entered the Post House and ordered a cup of coffee. It was bitter, weak. He drank it anyway and went out to the waiting room. He felt conspicuous.

Joe and Anita came. They walked like somnambulists, their eyes open but sightless, their feet leaden. Shank told them they were going to Chicago. They nodded vacantly.

Anita sat on a hard wooden bench and stared at nothing. Joe took a paperback novel from his blue jeans and began to read.

The bus left on time. They were on it, nervous, waiting, headed for Chicago. The night was black and the sky was starless. The bus raced to Chicago and they raced with it. It went fast but not fast enough.

"Joe—"

He looked up. Anita was speaking to him. She had said hardly a word in days. She had lowered a copy of the *Chicago Tribune* to talk directly to him.

"He killed a man, Joe. In Cleveland. That's how he got the money for the tickets. He stuck up a man and shot him six times in the back. He used the same gun he got from the cop in New York, He killed him, Joe."

Joe had guessed as much. He wished Anita hadn't said anything. It was bad this way. Best to forget it, to sink gracefully into immobility, to bury your head in the sand. Shank was out now. They were waiting for him in the hotel room that in effect reproduced the rooms in Buffalo and Cleveland.

Now Shank was looking for someone named Bunky. Bunky would give them money, or a connection, or something. Bunky would save the day. Then the trio would be safe again; the three could stop running. Joe wondered how it would feel to stop running. They had been running for a long time.

"He's a killer," Anita persisted. "He didn't have to kill that man, Joe. He didn't have to kill the cop, either. He could have let him live. He meant to kill him. You don't shoot someone six times unless you want to kill him. He's a murderer."

"We're all murderers."

"Maybe," she said. "Maybe we are. I don't know any more. We were going to live clean, Joe. Do you remember? Our own apartment on 19th Street near Gramercy Park. All by ourselves. You were supposed to have a good job and I would be keeping the apartment nice for you. So wonderful. It would have been so wonderful."

"A dream, Anita."

She looked at him.

"A dream," he continued in a monotone. "Everything's a dream. No apartment, no clean. No anything. Just running."

"Can we ever stop?" Anita's voice climbed higher.

"I don't know."

"They'll catch us, Joe. He must know that. You can't get away from murder by crossing a state line. You just can't do it. They'll catch us."

"Maybe."

"And then what? How far can we run? How fast? They'll kill us. Just like he killed the cop. And just like he killed the man in Cleveland."

Joe was silent.

"What next, Joe?"

"I think he wants to get out of the country."

She laughed. Her laughter was low, bitter, humorless.

"Of course," she said. "Out of New York, out of the state, out of the country. Run like a rabbit and wind up dead as a doornail. Where to?"

"Mexico."

She was all eyebrow.

"I think that's what he wants to do," he explained. "Connect with this Bunky. A guy he knew in Frisco or something. Connect with Bunky and get some bread together. Then head for Mexico. He thinks we'll be safe in Mexico."

"Until he shoots somebody. Then what? Guatemala? Brazil? Spain? Where next?"

"If we get to Mexico—"

"We won't get to Mexico. We won't get anywhere. We'll be killed."

Joe lit a cigarette. "You can still walk out," he said "Shank won't mind, he won't even know where you went."

"Don't be silly."

"I'm not being silly," he said reasonably. "Chicago's a big town. You can walk out on us and disappear. You'll be safe. The cops know about you, sure. But they don't know who you are. They don't have your picture. You can find a niche for yourself and be safe."

"Do you want me to do that?"

He glanced away from her. "I don't know. I want you to be safe. I don't want you to get hurt."

"Joe—"

"I really don't know," he said. "I think I...this is silly, Anita. So silly."

"Go ahead, Joe."

"I still love you, Anita. Isn't that silly? All washed up, the whole world, all falling in. And I just plain love you. I don't understand it."

"I love you, Joe."

"Don't talk silly. I ruined you, loused you up. You had a life."

"It was an empty life."

"This one's worse."

"Maybe. Maybe not. Maybe everything is the way it is and we can't do anything about it."

"Run, Anita. Before he gets back. We'll make out. Shank and I. We'll manage."

"I can't, Joe."

"Leave me, Anita. I'm no good. I can't move. So I'm impotent without you—so what? Leave me."

"I can't, Joe. I can't."

He took her in his arms. "There ought to be a way out," he said. "Some way. There honest-to-God ought to. This is a mess."

She stroked his forehead. He was sweating.

"What do we do, baby?" Joe said, hopelessly.

"I guess we stick together."

"But how do we get out of this?"

"I wish I knew," she said. "God in heaven, I wish I knew."

They held each other and waited for Shank.

Shank's entrance was something special.

The door swung open. A second or two later Shank came through, his shoulders hunched, his white face more pale than usual. His eyes had a hunted look.

He closed the door, slid the bolt home. He turned to face them. The smile on his lips did not include his eyes.

"I found Bunky," he said.

They stared at him.

"It was tough," Shank said. "Had to turn the town upside-down. Big city, Chicago. I figured Bunky would be on the North Side. I combed that North Side. Went to all the hip hangouts, all the places a cat like Bunky would probably hang. Took time. Too much time."

"What happened?"

"I found him."

"And—"

Shank sighed. "Good old Bunky," he said. The smile grew but the eyes became more dead than ever. "He was glad to see me. Auld lang syne. That type of scene."

They waited.

"Something funny," he said. "Never would have expected it. Big change in Bunky. Fundamental difference from old Bunky. Big change."

Why didn't he get to the point? Anita and Joe wondered. He had connected with Bunky. The three could leave the country. Why did he have to drag it out forever?

"Funny," Shank said. "You know what it is about Bunky? Funny. It makes a poem."

They stared at him.

"Bunky is a junkie," he said. "Bunky is a junkie with a forty-pound monkey. It rhymes, dig? Isn't that funny? Isn't that the funniest thing you ever heard?"

11

"Junkie Bunky," Shank said. "No good at all to me. Horse is his whole life. Forty dollars a day. Forty dollars a day to put in his arm. He couldn't give me a connection."

"What then?"

A wider grin. "But don't panic. He told me the way. The way to Mexico. There's a plane making the trip once a week."

"You need some kind of a passport," Joe said softly.

"Not for this plane, baby. This is a private plane. It goes straight to Monterrey. From Chicago to Monterrey. Makes three stops at private airfields. Carries a dozen passengers, no more. You don't need anything like a passport for this one, baby. All you need is money."

"How much?"

"Two hundred a person."

"That's six hundred dollars."

"You add good, baby."

"How the hell can we get six hundred dollars?"

"Easy."

"Easy? Are you going to kill some more men, Shank? Shoot more old men in alleys?"

"It made the paper, huh?"

"It made the paper. And they traced the gun. They know it's us, Shank."

"I figured they would."

"So no more hold-ups, Shank. You can't pull a hold-up without a gun. Right?"

"Right as rain, Joe, baby. You've got a head on your neck. You truly do."

"Then how?"

Shank found a cigarette, placed it between his lips. He took a pack of matches, ripped one out and struck it. He lit the cigarette and dragged on it.

"Same way Bunky feeds his habit," he said. "Bunky uses almost three big bills a week. That's a lot of bread. And he gets it."

"How?"

"He's got a stable of girls, man. Three of them. Good little girls. Hustling girls. Working girls. Fly chicks. They take good care of Bunky. They go out and earn a habitful of money."

The message was beginning to sink in.

"We've got an asset," Shank said. "A natural resource. We've got little Anita. She can take care of us, Joe, baby. We carried her this far. Now she can carry us a little bit of the way. She can go wiggle her behind and carry us all the way to Mexico."

"I won't do it," Anita said, her tones flat.

Shank looked at her. She was standing up now, fear and disgust in her eyes. Shank walked to her, put his hand on her shoulder. She tried to shrink away, but his hand held.

"Sure you will," he said.

"No."

"Yes."

"No—"

"You listen to me," he said. "You shut your mouth and listen. They're going to kill us. All three of us. Strap us in the chair and turn on the juice. We'll die. Die for murder."

"You did the murders," she said. "You killed the cop. You shot the old man. I read in the paper the old man had three children. A wife and three children."

"So they'll get his insurance."

"You bastard!"

He laughed. A loud laugh. But he did not take his hand from her shoulder.

"You took my money," Shank said. "And you ran with me. Both of you. You were there when I killed the cop. And I killed the old man for you, for both of you. I could have run alone. I had enough money to make Chicago. I killed so you could come with me. So don't pin it on me, little girl. It doesn't work that way."

"Shank—"

She stopped. She had nothing to say. She could only stare at him and listen to him.

"Now you'll hustle," he told her. "We need six hundred dollars. Sounds like a lot of money. It's not that much. Say you get ten bucks a trick. It's only sixty tricks. You can handle twenty a day easy. Just quick tricks. Fast and easy and simple. Three days and we're ready to roll. Plane leaves in four days. So we can't miss. All you have to do is turn your tricks."

"I'm no whore."

Easy laughter rolled out of Shank.

"Whoever said you were?" he said. "I'm not telling you to make a profession out of it, baby. Just sixty times. Just sixty quick tricks to save us all. That's all, Anita. Maybe less, if you can get some guys to go more than ten bucks. Say, twenty. And the more tricks you turn, the faster you're done. And then—"

"You filthy son of a—"

"You'll do it, Anita. You'll do it whether you like it or not. Because it's the only way."

She tried to imagine herself as a prostitute. She pictured herself walking the streets, picking up men, taking their money and letting them use her body as a mute receptacle for their lust. She thought about the last thing he had suggested, the twenty dollar tricks, and she thought she was going to be sick to her stomach.

"Don't play virgin with me, Anita."

She turned to Joe, "Joe," she said. "I can't do it, Joe. Do you want me to do it? Do you want me to be a whore, Joe? Is that what you want?"

Joe's eyes were filled with pain.

"Tell me," she said. "Tell me to whore for you and I

will. Tell me that's what you want and I'll do it. I can't think straight any more, Joe. I thought I was your woman. I thought I was just for you. But tell me to do it and I'll do it. You tell me, Joe."

Joe stood up. His body uncoiled slowly and he stood up, his eyes on Shank.

"No," he said.

"Joe—" Shank started.

"No," he repeated. "Think of some other way, Shank. Some cleaner way."

"It's the only way."

"You better find another. She's my woman. She's not a hustler. Not now and not ever. So find another way."

Shank looked first at Joe, then at Anita, then at Joe again. He began to laugh.

"Your chick? That's funny, man. Too funny. You don't know how funny it is."

"What do you mean?"

"I mean I made it with her, baby. Back in New York. Right on your own little bed, man. So don't play possessive papa with me, baby. She's nobody's chick at all. And she can hustle and get us to Mexico like I said."

Joe went white.

"Is it true, Anita?" he said in a beaten voice.

Her voice was soft. "He made me, Joe. He made me do it. I didn't want to."

"Go on."

Joe's eyes were on Shank, cold. He listened to what she had to say.

"He made me, Joe. He…beat me up. He hurt me. And he was going to cut me with his knife. I was afraid. He…he raped me."

"You never told me."

"I was afraid."

Something happened to Joe. Something inside. He turned on Shank and his eyes were on fire.

"You son of a bitch!"

"Easy, baby."

"You rotten—"

"Cool! It don't change a thing, Joe. It's the same scene all across the board. Now she can hustle, you dig? Now she can earn some bread and—"

"No."

Shank sensed something. He knew that Joe was not kidding now. He shoved the girl and she skidded across the room.

"Back off, Joe."

But Joe moved forward.

Shank's hand dropped to his pocket. The knife came out in a single fluid motion. He held it in his right hand, his finger poised on the button.

"Back off."

"Drop it."

"I don't want to cut you, Joe. I don't want to hurt you. You better let it alone, man. It happened a long time ago. It's ancient history. We got to swing together or we both lose."

"You'll have to kill me."

"Don't make it tough, Joe."

"It's going to be tough. Very tough."

Shank nodded. His finger pressed on the button. The knife blade shot forward, six inches of glistening steel.

Shank rubbed his thumb back and forth across the face of the blade. His eyes were on Joe.

Joe kept coming.

Shank moved the knife back and forth like the head of a cobra about to strike, He moved around in a little dance. His eyes were on Joe's face.

Joe backed away and Shank moved in, the knife moving back and forth, ready. Joe moved to the side of the bed. His hand dropped, gripped a pillow.

Shank lunged with the knife and Joe swung with the pillow. The timing was perfect. The knife slashed into the pillow and feathers filled the room, fluttering to the floor. Joe yanked on the pillow, dropped it and crashed a fist to the side of Shank's jaw.

Shank staggered. His head dropped and Joe caught it on the way down with both hands. He cupped the head, pushed it down, raised a knee to meet it.

Teeth gave way.

Shank sank to the floor. He started to raise himself on his knees. Then Joe kicked him in the face and he fell down again. The feathers settled over him. Some of the feathers were red from the blood from his mouth.

This time he stayed down.

Shank regained consciousness some ten minutes later. Joe was standing over him, knife in hand. Joe's other arm was around Anita.

"You won," Shank said slowly. "But it doesn't change a thing."

"You think not?"

"We're in the same spot," Shank said. "We're running. We still need six hundred dollars. So you beat me. Solid. But we're married, baby. You can't cut me out."

"Anita," Joe said. "Go pick up the phone."

"You calling somebody? I don't get it, baby. Who are you calling?"

Shank did not understand. But Joe did, finally. Everything was very clear now. It all fit in place.

And Joe knew everything was going to be all right. He had found some portion of himself, a portion that had been lost for a long, long time. Not too long, though. The portion was still there—and functioning.

Joe looked at Anita and loved her. He knew it was going to be all right with them now. From here on in everything was going to be all right.

"Pick up the phone," he repeated. "Dial the operator. Dial 0."

"Joe—" Shank began.

He told Shank to shut up. "Tell the operator you want the police, Anita," he went on. "Tell them to come over here right away. Tell them you've got a murderer trapped."

"They'll fry us all, Joe. They'll cool the three of us," Shank promised.

"Just you," Joe said. "Just you."

"You'll go to jail."

"Maybe. But we'll get out. You'll fry but we'll get out. And we'll be alive then. We won't have to run any more."

"You're crazy!" Shank said in a high-pitched voice.

Joe flicked a glance at Shank. Anita was talking to the police on the telephone, her voice very calm.

"You're the one who's crazy," he told Shank. "I'm sane. I'm sane again. It's been a long time, but I'm sane again."

Anita finished the call. She walked to Joe's side, and the three waited for the police to come.

But it was not a trio the police found.